Teolinda Gersão

The Word Tree

Translated by Margaret Jull Costa

Dedalus

M|C
Ministério da Cultura

DG
LB
DIRECÇÃO-GERAL
DO LIVRO E DAS
BIBLIOTECAS

IC

INSTITUTO
CAMÕES
PORTUGAL
MINISTÉRIO DOS NEGÓCIOS ESTRANGEIROS

Dedalus would like to thank the Directorate for Books and Libraries / Portugal and the Camoes Institute for their assistance in producing this book. Obra publicada com o apoio do Instituto Camões – Portugal

Published in the UK by Dedalus Limited,
24–26 St Judith's Lane, Sawtry, Cambs, PE28 5XE
email: info@dedalusbooks.com
www.dedalusbooks.com

ISBN 978 1 903517 88 8

Dedalus is distributed in the USA by SCB Distributors,
15608 South New Century Drive, Gardena, California 90248
email: info@scbdistributors.com   web: www.scbdistributors.com

Dedalus is distributed in Australia by Peribo Pty Ltd.
58 Beaumont Road, Mount Kuring-gai N.S.W. 2080
email: info@peribo.com.au

Dedalus is distributed in Canada by Disticor Direct-Book Division
695 Westney Road South, Suite 14, Ajax, Ontario, LI6 6M9
email: ndalton@disticor.com   web: www.disticordirect.com

Publishing History
First Published in Portugal in 1996
First Dedalus edition in 2010

A Árvore das Palavras copyright © Teolinda Gersão 1996
Translation copyright © Margaret Jull Costa 2010

The right of Teolinda Gersão to be identified as the author and Margaret Jull Costa to be identified as the translator of this work has been asserted by them in accordance with the Copyright, Designs and Patent Acts, 1988

Printed in Finland by WS Bookwell
Typeset by RefineCatch Limited, Bungay, Suffolk

THE AUTHOR

Teolinda Gersão is the author of 12 novels and short-story collections, which have been translated into eleven different languages. Her work has brought her many prizes, including the Pen Club Prize for best novel (twice), the Literature Prize from the International Critics' Literary Association and the Grand Prix for Novel and Short-Story from the Portuguese Writers' Association. *The Word Tree* is the first of her novels to be published in English.

THE TRANSLATOR

Margaret Jull Costa has been a literary translator from Portuguese and Spanish for over twenty years, translating such authors as Fernando Pessoa, José Saramago and Javier Marías. In 2008 she won the PEN/Book-of-the-Month Translation Award and the Oxford Weidenfeld Translation Prize for her version of Eça de Queiroz's masterpiece *The Maias*, and in 2009 she was awarded the Valle-Inclán Spanish Translation Prize for *The Accordionist's Son* by Bernardo Atxaga.

TRANSLATOR'S ACKNOWLEDGEMENTS

I would like to thank Teolinda Gersão for making the translation of her novel such a uniquely pleasurable, collaborative experience.

DEDALUS AFRICA

Dedalus Africa aims to introduce to the English-speaking world outstanding literary fiction either from or about Africa.

We begin with Teolinda Gersão's evocation of growing up in Africa, a novel about what can happen when Europe and Africa meet.

This is our starting point.

1

To reach the backyard you had to go through the narrow kitchen door. And although it's true that the kitchen was dark, you could still see all the objects in it, the aluminium pans and fat pots, the jugs and enamel bowls, the old white oven with its brass rings, the big table with the marble top on which some piece of crockery had always been left out by mistake. But you tended to ignore the kitchen, you didn't really look at it, but ran in the direction of the yard, as if you were being sucked towards it by the light, and you staggered a little as you went through the door, because you were blinded for a few seconds, and only the smell and the heat guided your first steps, the smell of earth, grass and over-ripe fruit that wafted to you on the warm wind like the breath of some living animal.

Everything in the back yard danced: the broad leaves of a banana tree, the flowers and leaves of the hibiscus, the still tender branches of the jacaranda, the blades of grass that grew like weeds and against which, after a certain point, we gave up the struggle.

It was only when you lay down in the grass that you noticed how slender the jacaranda leaves were, sweeping the sky, and how the sun was a blue and gold eye watching, blinding all others, so that only he could see; up there above the garden and the house, the sun was the only seeing eye.

But as I said, you didn't need eyes to see because you could do that even with them shut, through your closed lids inundated with light – the chicken wire on the hen-coop at the back of the yard, the wall, the tiled roof of the house, the windows, the dark doorway, always open, the balcony on the first floor, where, at the end of the day, Laureano would sit drinking a beer. You didn't need eyes to see because you knew everything, it was yours, you didn't even need to hope or wish for anything because things simply happened of their own accord and came to meet you – and so, for example, at the end of the day, you just had to raise your head to see Laureano sitting out on the balcony.

Then night fell, like a glass of dark beer spilled by the sky. Or like an eyelid closing. Because the dusk came quickly – well, there wasn't really any dusk to speak of, there was no gradual transition: it was either dark or light.

Down below, while Laureano was sitting on the balcony, the garden grew like a wild thing. A sorghum plant would sprout from seed dropped by accident or put out for the birds; a clandestine beanstalk would shoot up among the daisies; brambles and nettles and nameless weeds grew among the golden-shower orchids and the bauhinia; any seed carried by the wind eventually burgeoned into green leaves licked by the summer rains. And Amélia would say, frowning: 'The garden's turning into a jungle.' And she'd slam the window shut.

It wasn't a garden, it was a wilderness, which you either loved or hated; there were no half measures, because you couldn't compete with it. It was there and it surrounded us, and you were either part of it or you weren't. Amélia wasn't. Or didn't want to be. That's why she continued to try and tame it. 'I want this swept,' she would say to Lóia. No fruit peel could be left lying on the ground, no seed or stone could be thrown down. 'That kind of thing might be all right in the shanty-towns,' she would say about anything that displeased her, 'but not here.'

And so the house was divided in two, the White House and the Black House. The White House belonged to Amélia, the Black House to Lóia. The yard surrounded the Black House. I belonged to the Black House and to the yard.

'You have to be careful,' Amélia said, 'alert. Things look

10

all right on the surface, but the city is rotten and rife with contagion. It was built on swampland, you know.'

When anyone fell ill, she always assumed it was one of the old fevers that periodically returned and left people weak and hollow-eyed, as if sucked dry by evil spirits. The swamp, or the memory of the swamp, which she had never known because it had ceased to exist almost a century before, seemed to besiege her with nightmare visions, as if the putrid, marshy water was still there, close by. And she herself would always accompany the sanitary inspector and the local black official, who made the occasional rare visit, wearing yellow armbands, to poke around in the yard, spraying the corners and the walls with a foul-smelling chemical that was supposed to eliminate or repel mosquitos.

In the Black House no one was afraid of mosquitos, or, for that matter, of anything else. In the Black House things sang and danced. The hens would escape from the coop and walk all over any washing that happened to fall from the line, blithely shitting wherever they pleased. Lóia would shout at the hens and shoo them away, but then, kneeling down, she would burst out laughing and scrub at the soiled washing with a bar of soap and rinse it with a watering-can full of water. She obviously enjoyed doing these things because she was always laughing and never really bothered to keep the hens locked up, and so they would shit on the clothes again, and she would wash them again – the water fell like rain from the spout of the watering-can that swung in her hand as she carried it, and on the way from tap to clothes, it revived the flowers too.

And so the flowers never died for very long, but bloomed again; all it took was for Lóia to go back and forth a few times with the watering-can in her hand and the water was transformed into rain. And one day, while she sat on a bench at the entrance to the yard, she even brought a cockerel back to life, having first killed it on the kitchen table and plunged it, plucked, into boiling water.

It lay on her bloodstained apron, beak open and wings outspread, looking like a sack of jugo beans. If it had slipped from her grasp, it would have made quite a noise as it fell. But she kept a firm grip; she pulled out the feathers and threw them over her head. As the wind caught them, she sat surrounded by a cloud of soft fluff that hovered about her and took time to fall once again to earth, while the cockerel turned into a fat, roundish, yellow, wingless thing that appeared triumphantly that night on the table, having first vanished into the gaping maw of the oven.

The following morning, though, she produced it from her apron and put it back in the chicken-run. And then you could see how she had put the bones together and covered them with that thick skin, yellow with fat and with little pimples where the feathers had been, and how easy it had been for her to stick each feather into its allotted place and skilfully reshape the little cockerel as if it were made of clay, and replace feet, claws, beak, eyes, one on either side, and finally the crest on top of its head.

Lóia opens his eyes by lifting his fallen lids, smooths his feathers, and blows into his beak. The cockerel lifts his neck, flutters his wings and finally opens his eyes. Now he's standing up on the table, crowing.

Laureano belongs to the Black House too. He's not afraid of mosquitos and he himself planted a castor-oil tree at the bottom of the yard. The cat Simba, which he brought home one day in his jacket pocket, sleeps on the carpet beside his chair at siesta time, on the days when he comes back for lunch, which is most days. Laureano doesn't really sleep in the after-noon, he dozes, sitting in the reclining chair with the broad arms, and which we call his aviator's chair.

The best moment, though, is the night-time, before I go to sleep, when he picks up a music box that has a dancing cat on the lid. It's a most surprising animal. Dressed in a satin doublet and a flounced shirt with a lace jabot, he holds an arched garland of flowers above his head while he dances in his high-heeled blue shoes. Everything about him intrigues and fascinates me, because he's a most unusual cat, of whom you would never think, as you would of Simba, that he was a cousin to the wild cat and still knows a lot about the jungle.

Laureano turns the handle and the cat twirls round to the music, whose light, tinny notes sound vaguely like a marimba. Questions occur to me – why is he dressed like that and why does he wear those shoes? – but I don't say anything because I want to listen and I'll have fallen asleep by the time he finishes his dance.

In exchange for that cat and his music, I'll play a game with you. When you arrive home in the afternoon and you call out as you come through the door: Giiii-taaa . . . only the silence answers, the house seems empty and sleepy. Because I'm not here, as I was at lunchtime, waiting for you by the window, I've transformed myself into a small animal that has crept away behind the cupboard on furtive feet. And you have stopped being you and are now a large animal creeping unstoppably ever closer.

I feel you walking, invisible, past the furniture in the hall-way, pushing open the living-room door, sniffing the air, peering under tables and behind curtains, while I almost disappear into the shadows, heart beating faster and faster, conscious that nothing will give me greater pleasure than the moment of near-terror when you find me, when you are still not yet you, nor even a man, but the unknown, the animal, the monster, bursting into the house and violating the old order.

Being found is a death, a joy, the crossing of a line. That's why I scream, out of terror, pleasure and fear. And then you pick me up and I know I'm at your mercy and that, like a vanquishing beast, you could carry me off into the depths of the jungle. That moment is a small joyful death. You triumph over me and I disappear into your arms as if I were being devoured. Then suddenly I'm alive, on the other side of a gigantic wave.

And now you're you again, a man, the beloved man of the house. I see your face, your body, especially your eyes, and I don't know how an animal – or some evil thing – could ever have taken your place, because now you're as familiar to me as the wind and the rain.

Then there follows much laughter and great peace, at the dizzying moment when the formless terror shatters and is transformed once more into you. And I laugh with pleasure because I was the one who invented the game. It was me, crouching very still behind the door, who changed you into an animal, when the blood beat so hard in my chest that my heart almost leapt into my mouth. I'm the one who allows myself to be discovered and who turns you back into a man again.

At that point, I feel such tenderness for you and such pity for being so slow to understand, because it's just a game, but you'll never realise that and will always fall into it as if into a well, and I'll stay up above, laughing, and that laughter will be like a stone thrown into the water, sending out ripple upon ripple.

And then I close my eyes and I know that I'm going to fall in too, that this game is carrying me, like water, into the luminous depths of the well. Even though I know it's a game, which I invent and reinvent every day, each time you come home. A repeated game, like the sun or the moon at the window.

Yes, everything in the yard danced, the leaves, the earth, the spots of sunlight, the branches, the trees, the shadows. They danced and had no limits, nothing did, not even your own body, which grew in all directions and was as big as the world. Your body was the tree and the wind. It could touch the sky simply by raising its head a little, swaying on the dancing wind; life was a dance then, and just placing one foot in front of the other set the body celebrating: everything was in the body and of the body, the shrill cries of the birds flying overhead, the hot breath of the African summer, the great night dotted with stars. But the infinite didn't frighten or surprise us really; it was a simple idea, the certainty that we could grow up as high as the sky.

And maybe that was how we came to know all the secrets – the world was familiar and we knew it down to its tiniest details, knew the curved shell of the snail and the sound of the rain on leaves. The sunlight on the wall and the high trill of the cicadas. The taste of the earth on the tongue and the sickly savour of ants.

The yard and the house had no limits either, they were large enough to contain everything. You could hear, when you were lost in thought, the stealthy steps of wild beasts, and when you slept, you could feel their breath on your face. And when you slept deeply like that, your feet and arms joined with their wild bodies and you suddenly knew how to leap from branch to branch, even, when necessary, over the torrents and waterfalls of dreams.

Then you would sigh, breathing through your half-open mouth into the sheets, you would turn your head on the pillow, but you were still running through the forest, alighting noiselessly on large paws, sniffing the warm night air, alert to the slightest rustle among the leaves. You would travel long paths in the forest and in the night. Then you would drink, at last, from the long-sought water. You would lower your head until your lips touched the surface and then be off again, light-footed as an antelope.

Or you would plunge into the water in order to slake your thirst more quickly, and then your body felt as muddy and contented as a submerged pachyderm.

All night you wandered free and could change your skin at any moment. You could be the swift body of the polecat and eat the juicy fruit of the *mampsincha*, or you could sniff the wind with the angry snout of the hyena.

You could be everything, and in the morning you returned. You opened your eyes, but, even with eyes wide open, nothing changed. You leapt out of bed with the cloven hooves of the zebra and, in front of the bathroom mirror, you brushed your sharp rabbit teeth. Lóia would place milk and fruit on the table, and you'd devour it all like a famished animal, then leave, tail wagging.

The day didn't interrupt your dreams. You could sleep with your eyes open, and life was pleasurable, as easy as playing and dreaming. You could spread wide your arms and shout: I'm alive, but there was no need for such exultant, exaggerated gestures; things were so close and simple that you barely noticed them. For example, you would go out of the kitchen door, unaware that you were crossing a threshold. There was no separation between spaces, no intervals separating the days. Because your body joined earth to sky.

Lóia was outside in the yard and everything else was in movement. That's how I imagine her, immobile, fixed to one spot, with everything else revolving around her.

The water gushes from the tap into the wash-tub, into which she throws the towels and sheets, then the water drains slowly away, creamy with soap, when she pulls out the plug. She wrings out the washing, soaking her feet in the process, so that they look as if they were covered in milk up to the ankles, all the while holding her baby Ló with one arm and adjusting her *capulana*, the broad strip of cloth that binds the child to her. Lóia always has a child with her, either at her breast or on her back.

This, apparently, is exactly how she turned up at the house one day, clutching Orquídea. She stopped warily at the door. 'Is this where they need a wetnurse?' she asked, without letting go of Orquídea.

'Come in, come in,' says Amélia impatiently – so impatient that her milk has dried up completely and her tongue too, as if everything in her had become all thinness and haste – and then immediately closes the door. 'Come in. The creature won't stop screaming and I've been expecting you since yesterday. Didn't Fana pass on my message?'

But Lóia is in no hurry because Orquídea is in no hurry either; she's sucking and sighing, making the sounds of a small sated animal. In the kitchen, Amélia shudders with disgust. 'You'll have to disinfect your breasts with alcohol, otherwise Gita might catch something.' But Lóia refuses to apply any disinfectant to her nipples, and Gita catches the very worst of all contagions: she becomes as black as Lóia and Orquídea.

Lóia puts a baby to each breast and sits in the kitchen or in the yard. And I take on the same smell as Orquídea, acquire the same firm, pliable flesh, plump but not fat, covered by a skin as soft as silk. Lóia never leaves us, sometimes even staying with us when we sleep. She always has one of us (usually the one who can't sleep) close to her body, secure in the *capulana*, and that's how she cooks, scrubs the floor, sweeps the house, does the laundry, lights the fire, scales the fish, irons the clothes, and dusts the knickknacks with the blue and yellow feather duster.

Up on the balcony, Laureano smiles. He knows I'm not going to die now, I who had been as pale as wax with arms as thin as Amélia's sewing thread.

Lóia smiles too. A slow smile that hovers on her thick lips, revealing her teeth and gums, white teeth with gaps between them.

The closed curtains, the shadowy warmth of the bedroom, the clothes draped over the chair, the hushed voice of Lóia when it's time for our afternoon nap: 'Sh, sh.' The door slowly closing, Simba's erect tail about to be trapped, only to be withdrawn unhurriedly and at the very last moment.

I used to look at Orquídea in the dim light as if I were

looking in a mirror. She was the same size as me and identical in every respect. And above us Lóia would be saying 'Sh, sh', tucking in the sheet and closing the door.

All day I was her sister. We're sitting beneath the jacaranda tree and I cry 'Orquíiiiidea' and clutch her to me. She lets me hug her until she's breathless, then picks up fistfuls of earth and flings them into the air. We bat our arms about, closing our eyes and brushing the earth from our hair.

Then I go over to Lóia and say: 'I want hair like Orquídea's, in little braids round my head.'

Lóia removes her hands from the wash-tub and bursts out laughing. 'Wait, wait.'

She divides my hair into clumps about the thickness of a strand of wool, and onto each one she threads a pierced seed or a glass bead, then plaits them together as if she were embroidering. 'Wait, wait,' she keeps saying, when I wriggle impatiently, my head on her aproned lap.

The result is astonishing: I look exactly like Orquídea. I shake my head, tremulous with laughter. The braids bob about, but stay sticking out, swaying like insect antennae, except that there are ten of them not two, distributed around my head. I embrace my image, who follows me everywhere: Orquídea.

Amélia, however, doesn't like the way I look at all. 'Get rid of those braids this instant,' she says, opening the door of her sewing-room.

Happiness, every morning, like a bird beating at the window. And the sun was the head of a giant sunflower.

'Follow my paths,' said the snail shell, and I traced with my fingertip the dark line that set off from one point and became a wide circle, which, just as it was about to close, became another and another, none of which ever ended or closed.

'Come with me,' said the ant, disappearing into the earth.

'Sing louder,' said the cicada.

'Come inside me,' said the tree.

'I'll carry you with me,' said the wind.

The water dripped from the tap and formed a small puddle in the flower bed; the water falling from above woke up the water that had accumulated below, and the drops danced like ballerinas.

'So–so–so–so,' said the water as it fell.

And the little puddle repeated, singing:

'So–so–so–so,' on four different notes, two quick, sharp notes, one after the other, in between two slower, more hesitant ones.

We used to sit for a long time under the tree, leaning against its trunk, and, as I said, we would become trees ourselves. Or even become birds, although flying was a bit more difficult. But being things was easy. Because suddenly you held in your hand the root of everything living. Then your first ear would open and start to hear the wind. Then, after a long time, your second ear would open and you would start to hear the rain. And you had a lot of other ears that could hear your blood and the voices of other creatures, other things.

At that time, we knew everything and could issue orders to the world:

'Wake up, yeast, up you get.'

'Stop blowing, wind, just crouch down on the roof or spend the night cross-legged under the porch.'

'Sit down on the edge of the bed, death, and don't carry off in your bag that person who's about to die, not just yet, give him a little more time, a piece the size of a palm leaf.'

And in the winking of an eye night came and morning returned.

'You can't trust the blacks,' Amélia says. 'Because they hate us and wish us ill. They put the evil eye on us and can bring us illness or even death. Yes, your friend, your own friend can cause you to die.'

'She doesn't like me,' says Lóia about Amélia. 'She has a hard heart.'

But of Laureano she says: 'He has a big heart.' And she smiles, showing her bright white teeth and turning to look at him.

Amélia lives in the sewing-room, bent over the machine on the back of which is written: P f a f f, in large letters widely spaced. In the corridor you can hear its irritating, monotonous hum, interrupted, now and then, by a thread being broken or, every so often, by the keen metallic sound of scissors falling.

Usually Amélia breaks the thread with her fingers or puts it between her teeth and gives it a sharp tug before putting it back in her mouth to thread the needle.

She doesn't use scissors to cut the thread, which makes sense, given how thin it is, especially in comparison with what always seemed to me the excessively large scissors. I gaze in amazement at the deft way her small, quick hands wield those scissors, which look to me as big as pruning shears.

Amelia, however, is not intimidated when it comes to cutting cloth: she makes a line with ruler and chalk down the whole length of the fabric and then the scissors follow that line, not so much cutting as tearing the cloth, until it has parted the cloth in two.

Above the equally enormous cutting table, hanging from the ceiling, is a lamp with a white enamel shade; the lamp is on a pulley with a weight in the shape of a grenade. When the daylight begins to fade, Amélia lights the lamp by turning on a porcelain switch next to the bulb, and then, reaching up above her head, she quickly raises or lowers the lamp to the desired height. And she does this without taking her eyes off her work, on which she is concentrated, lips pursed and with a frown line that runs vertically down the middle of her forehead and ends between her eyebrows.

She sighs, bent over the table, occasionally putting in pins that she takes from a small round cushion fixed to her shoulder. Sometimes she grips the pins in her mouth, and the sharp points appear between her teeth, as if they were part of them.

'Please don't do that,' Laureano would plead. 'It would be certain death if you swallowed one. I mean what would happen if you coughed or sneezed, have you ever thought of that?'

But she took no notice and continued to put the pins in her mouth and to talk through clenched teeth to anyone who came for a fitting.

'Yes, yes,' said the client, who, more often than not, was Elejana Miranda. 'It needs taking in a bit there. And there. And there. And there.'

She would twirl round in front of the mirror, half-wary, half-pleased, then take a step or two so that the hem of the dress swayed.

Amélia, kneeling on the carpet, measured the dress at the front and the back.

'A bit more off the hem?'

Elejana hesitated. 'No,' she said at last. She still felt that the dress went up a bit at the front.

Amélia shook her head, still kneeling on the carpet. She had measured it, and it was exactly the same. She showed her the tape-measure and went to fetch a gadget that squirted chalk round the hem, at the exact place, so that she could check the distance between floor and hem.

The client sighed again, unconvinced. 'Look, just make it a bit lower at the front,' she said peremptorily.

'All right,' said Amélia pulling out all the tacking stitches with a single tug.

Once Elejana had left, she let rip with her feelings:

'What needs trimming is your belly, you fat old thing,' she muttered, grabbing the scissors. 'It's all that fat that makes the dress go up at the front.'

Laureano is whistling in the bathroom, then singing to himself: 'O Laurindinha, come to the window', which I change to 'Laurentina':

'O Laurentina, come to the window,' we sing together, and he runs the sharp blade of the razor over his foam-covered cheek.

On Sundays, he lets me prepare the soap in a metal bowl and apply it to his face with a short-handled brush, which I can't dip into the bowl without getting my hands wet. Now, though, he has to go to work and is shaving himself in a hurry, his fingers deftly holding the two parts of the razor open and making regular downward strokes that clear a path through the foam on his cheeks; then he splashes his face with water and dries it on the towel, and he does all this so quickly that I suspect there must still be some foam left.

But there's no time to check, all I can do is put a few drops of the liquid from the green bottle on my hands and rub it on his face; it smells very strong and leaves on my hands and on the towel where I dry them the intense smell that will last all day. Then he says 'See you later' and leaves, almost at a run, pulling on his jacket as he goes down the stairs.

I wake up feeling thirsty halfway through my afternoon nap. 'I need to get some water from the fridge,' I think. I get up without making a sound, climbing over Orquídea.

I hear Amélia leaving the kitchen and going back into the sewing-room. There it is, there's the hum of the machine again. Amélia never takes a nap and she tells Lóia off whenever she catches her sitting in the yard, dozing.

I don't want Amélia to hear me and so I tiptoe past the door and go down the corridor to the kitchen that she left only moments before, the tap still dripping. Drops of water are falling ceaselessly, one after the other, into the sink. Nervous drops, full of hatred.

I don't want to hear them and so I rush over to turn the tap off properly. The sink is very high, though, and I have to drag the bench over and climb onto it, but up there everything's so uncertain, so unstable, and I still can't reach the tap and when I lean further over, I fall helplessly onto the floor.

Amélia pushes open the door, bumps into the bench, then picks me up, shouting:

'Stupid girl, stupid girl.'

Her hand comes down on me and rises, then falls, then rises again, as if it were never going to stop, and for a moment I feel nothing, just emptiness and me tumbling down a well, the walls giving way, the bench clattering to the floor again.

'Stupid girl, why can't you just sit still.'

Only later will I feel the pain and the fear, but for a long time there is only emptiness and Amélia's shouting going on and on.

Then she sits down on the floor and starts to cry.

That was what always happened in the end. Amélia would sit down on the floor and start to cry.

'She doesn't love me,' she would sob. 'My daughter, my own daughter.'

Lóia's large hands, as nimble as two right hands. She was never in a hurry and you would think, to see her lumbering around, that she couldn't possibly be an efficient worker. She had her own personal logic that disarmed or excluded all others. For example, she refused to learn how to tell the time, preferring to measure it by the position of the shadows in the yard. If we explained, pointing to the clock face, she would look at us and smile indulgently as if we'd gone mad. And if we moved the hands of the clock and, after further patient explanation, asked her: 'Right, what time is it now?' She would say whatever came into her head and escape to the kitchen.

She herself was a challenge to common logic because her huge, bulky body was out of keeping with the lightness of her movements or the gentleness of her gestures. The astonishing rapidity with which she tidied the house seemed equally at odds with the infinite tolerance she showed towards objects, as if she didn't want to offend them or force them to do anything, seeming, rather, to give them time to sort themselves out on their own, without her imposing any order on them at all, and then suddenly, as if by magic, all the household tasks would be done.

And what's more she would sing softly to herself, as if life were a song.

On the other hand, she would often sigh – 'Yotatanée!' – and complain about the chalk lines on the carpet, the needles scattered everywhere, the discarded shoes, the clothes stuffed willy-nilly into drawers. Because Amélia, apart from the sewing, for which she was paid, did no housework at all, not even bothering to hang up her clothes in the wardrobe.

'She has a heavy heart,' says Lóia. 'It beats lightly, but it's heavy. And cold as stone.'

'Why?' I ask, startled. 'Why?'

'Because she's dead. She's alive, but she's dead,' says Lóia.

Without Lóia we have no food, no clean dishes, no ironed clothes, no clean anything. And the house rapidly goes to rack and ruin.

This happens sometimes, when Lóia disappears for a few days without warning. Amélia rants and raves, hurls the dishcloth at the wall, and declares that she's going to hire a new cook and a washerwoman.

'You can't trust people like her,' she says over and over, in despair. 'They come when they want to, and when they don't want to, they just vanish. If she does this one more time, she's never darkening our door again.'

But Laureano won't let her get rid of Lóia. Because I couldn't bear to lose her, or Orquídea.

'If God doesn't want me dead, I'll come back,' Lóia tells me when she returns. 'Don't you be afraid.'

Deep down, Amélia doesn't want to lose Lóia either, which is why she puts up with her and with Orquídea and my closeness to them both. But as soon as their backs are turned, she complains that she can't even stand the smell of them and furiously flings open all the windows.

'They used to sing and dance around the tree,' says Lóia. Around the tree of the ancestors. They would offer sacrifices of flour in its honour, because that's where the children's spirits came from.

They used to sing and dance around the tree.

'The ancestors were spirits and gods. You asked them for good harvests, healthy cattle, a quiet life. People, lots of them, would come and sing, but that was far from here, near the river Incomati,' said Lóia.

They sang and the spirits listened.

Now you're home. The doors close noiselessly, the night hesitates for a moment at the window, on which we draw the curtain. Everything turns inwards, becomes intimate, dense, just like when you pause in the middle of doing something and can suddenly hear the rain.

The rest of the world fades, the town becomes a far-distant murmur, a diffuse shadow. I hear the sounds surrounding you, the noise of you distractedly dragging your aviator's chair nearer to the light. I see you from the door, concealed behind your newspaper. I see: feet, socks, cotton trousers, pale short-sleeved shirt. The watch on your left wrist, your elbow crooked, holding your newspaper. But right from the moment you arrived and even before that, you were always a presence, a whole, even when I wasn't looking at you.

And now that I've walked round behind your aviator's chair, I can see your dark hair, your head slightly bent, and the back of your neck, the place behind your ears on which the arms of your spectacles rest.

I hop towards you. The sole of my shoe thuds on the floor, but you continue reading, as if you hadn't heard. Pretending, pretending. But I only give you a short time before you have to choose between the newspaper and me. And because I know that you will always choose me, I laugh quietly as I hop round your chair.

Because I know for certain that you are good. And that is a very large certainty, like knowing that the earth turns, the sun rises, or that the seasons of the year follow one upon the other. You are good in the way that trees are trees and rain is rain. There is no need to think about these things because no one disputes the evidence.

Living is very easy, because I use you as the point from which to measure north and south. As long as you exist, the meridians arrange themselves in their proper positions and the oceans do not overflow. You're sitting in your aviator's chair and I am walking round it, I can come closer or move farther off, I can even turn my back on you and walk in the opposite direction, but I know that I won't get lost, because you will always be there at the end of each day, sitting and reading the newspaper. Every time I turn my head, you're there.

A good man is a light in the window. Things take on shape and solidity, brightness and colour, and I dance among them. It's because I'm safe that I have the freedom to dance, it's because I'm not afraid that I can improvise, it's because I know nothing about routine that I can surrender myself to the glow. That is what dance is, a more intense way of living. The trees dance, the leaves dance, the rain dances, the animals dance, the sun and the moon dance. All you have to do is allow yourself to be drawn into their circle, let yourself be sucked fearlessly into the great orbit of things. Then life begins to flow through us and to include us, and we bow our heads and say 'Yes' and we dance.

And now that I have hopped round the world, round your chair, I will allow you no more time, and I will jump into your lap, demolishing the newspaper. Like Simba the cat.

It's then, when you smile and let go of the open pages, that I can really look at you: the small face, the trim moustache, the thin, wire-rimmed glasses. I look at you bit by bit, as if I were remembering you, even though you're right there in front of me and I don't need to remember you – I look at you simply for the pleasure of looking at you – the round, wire-rimmed glasses, the sweat-stained shirt, in whose pocket I discover a small comb, with one tooth broken, your eyes, creased at the corners into fine lines, your white teeth, almost as white as Lóia's, shining beneath your moustache, the points of which turn up.

While you're talking, I think that something about your face reminds me of a rabbit – perhaps your slightly timid air, that could seem standoffish if I didn't know you so well, the light, almost furtive way that you walk about the house, the way in which you occasionally don't finish your sentences – because rabbits, people say, don't finish their sentences either, they leave them, as you do, hanging in the air. Out of slyness, people say, because a person gets along better if he doesn't explain himself fully and simply lets others guess what he's thinking, so that, later, he can change his mind according to the circumstances. But you don't do this in a calculating fashion, so it isn't there that your resemblance to rabbits lies – even though your ears are slender, and the end of your nose does twitch, making your glasses wobble slightly. Rabbits don't wear glasses, of course, which is another feature that distinguishes you from them. But then your skin is soft and hairy, although that hair is sparser and not as long as rabbit hair. Apart from on your head and your moustache.

But the real reason you remind me of a rabbit is because, in stories, rabbits are always the cleverest of creatures. The rabbit always gets the better of the lion, the wild boar, the elephant, the leopard and all the animals of the jungle. And because the rabbit is the strongest, he's the king.

Lóia is from Marracuene and her man, Zedequias, used to work in the mines in Jone, but he's come back here now and works down at the docks. He has saved from his days in the mines a battery-run radio that only works when you shake it hard or when, in despair, you bang it on the floor.

The children are shown to the moon when they're born, so that she will do them no harm. In the village of Marracuene, they lost one son when he was very small and another when he had already learned to walk.

The dead children get lost in the forest or the jungle, they look for the path home, but can't find it, because the dead, like lizards, have no sense of smell, which is why they can't find their way back.

She tells me these and other things while she's kneeling down, applying Cobra wax to the wooden floor.

At this point, Lóia no longer sleeps in our house, she leaves at the end of the day and returns in the morning, sometimes bringing Ló and Orquídea with her.

She can't have time to sleep, I think anxiously. She'll spend all night travelling home and by the time she gets there, it will be time to set off again. Because she's here in the morning, early. She opens my bedroom door, trips over Simba, who races for the stairs, and then draws the curtain. 'Wake up, miss, wake up.'

'Where do you live?' I ask.

And she says: 'Far away.' And she sighs.

'But where is "far away",' I ask, 'is it farther than Chamanculo, Avenida de Angola, Munhuana, Xipamanine, Mafalala? Farther than Estrada das Lagoas?'

She says again: 'Yes. Far away.' And sighs.

'We know nothing about the blacks,' says Amélia. 'And we can't go looking for them because we don't know where they live, they have no address, they live in vague, unnamed places, in straw-thatched huts that all look the same, in shanty-towns. Finding one of them is like looking for a needle in a haystack.'

Then came a day which was, perhaps, a very hot Christmas Eve. Laureano is looking in the pantry, filling a basket with whatever he can find, biscuits, chocolate, cakes and a bottle of wine, and he insists on carrying it to the bus for her, because she's still carrying Ló at her breast. Lóia doesn't want him to and protests mildly, smiling broadly – please, *patrão* – because she doesn't think it right that he should carry such a weight; with the hand not being held by Orquídea she tries to grab the handle, but he insists and we leave. Laureano, me, Lóia, Ló and Orquídea, a little family walking along. The trees are swaying above our heads, the air is cooler now, and we rediscover the joy of walking.

Sometimes, without warning, I grab both their hands and do a rapid somersault between them, landing back on my feet. This startles them for a moment, but then they laugh. Orquídea copies me and Lóia says: 'You're not girls, you're monkeys.' Then we run on ahead, me and Orquídea, and when we come back, we change places and walk on in a different order, hand-in-hand, Laureano, me, Orquídea, Ló and Lóia, Laureano, Orquídea, me, Ló and Lóia, Laureano, Orquídea, Ló, Lóia and me.

Until we reach the bus stop, in Largo João Albasini, and join the long queue of people waiting, although Laureano and I could easily leave, because we have done our duty, or his duty, by carrying the basket. But neither of us wants to leave, and so we wait too, although it's very hard to stay still for so long in the same place, and our tired bodies seek respite by shifting from one foot to the other. It was as if we thought – absurdly – that the fact of being there would make the rest of the journey easier for her, between the last stop and the place where she lives and where there will be no one to help her – or perhaps we thought nothing, and staying at the bus stop was simply the obvious thing to do, and it didn't occur to us to do anything else.

Until, finally, the number 13 bus arrives, in a cloud of dust, and stops in front of us, with a great roar of the engine. Inside, all the windows are full, all the spaces taken from floor to ceiling, apparently tiny figures sway about in the aisle, hanging on to the seats – men, old people, women, children, boys in faded shirts.

In the street, there is a muttering, an anxious murmur of people pushing and worrying whether there's going to be room for them or not; we're carried forward on a human wave, and then Lóia lets go of my hand and gets on the bus with Ló and Orquídea. I watch her grab the bar at the door and then wave, from among a sea of watching faces. The bus pulls out, churning up more dust and sounding as if it were about to fall apart at any moment, then moves further and further off until we lose sight of it. For a long moment, everything still seems to be happening: Lóia's hand letting go of mine to grab the bar at the door, the bus leaving, her wave, and then inside, in the middle of those swaying heads, her body, which looked almost small now, and the tiny faces of Ló and Orquídea, the glass in the window seeming to cut their faces in two.

Then everything disappears, as if by magic, and I'm left behind, in a cloud of dust. Night falls suddenly, we can barely make out the gangling silhouettes of the trees against the sky, the Earth is a dead and desolate planet, floating in space.

Perhaps that was when the dreams started – I would be walking through the forest with Lóia and she would suddenly head off along a path and disappear into the undergrowth.

'Lóóóiiiaa,' I called, trying to run after her, but unable even to walk because of the stabbing pain I felt each time I took a step and because my suddenly swollen foot no longer fitted in my shoe. 'Lóóóiiaa,' I called again, struggling onwards and whooping with joy when I caught sight of a blue and red scarf behind a bush. But when I got there, the scarf was nowhere to be seen. I sat down, barefoot, on the ground and realised that the reason I couldn't walk was that I had trodden on a thorn.

'Don't leave,' I say to her in the morning, putting my arms around her. 'Not ever.'

'Don't cry,' she says. 'Don't cry.'

She sits on the floor beside me and, with just a couple of quick movements of her hands, she makes me a rag doll out of the loose scraps and remnants from Amélia's sewing, from the buttons and rings, hooks and glass beads left lying around, and which are suddenly brought together to make a whole figure. I watch her fingers, fascinated, as if she were performing a magic trick, and I gaze at the doll in amazement because it seems so mysterious to me. A length of thread binds the different parts together, invisible, but strong enough to transform the doll into something almost alive. And this happened right before my eyes, emerged almost out of nothing. I saw it.

'I'm going to call her Ló,' I say, picking the doll up with both hands, 'because she looks just like her.'

I follow Lóia out into the yard, placing my feet in her footsteps. Where you go, I go, what you do, I do too. Even something really amazing. I mean it. I'll make a living doll. And if someone cuts her up, I'll stitch her back together with needle and thread so that she's whole again.

And suddenly I feel so happy and so strong that I dare to invent the story of the dead child. Someone, not an animal, not a spirit, someone who is no one, just a mouth, devours a child and chops it up. Lóia picks up the pieces and the cut-up child becomes whole again, just as the waning moon does, just as the dead cockerel sang once more in the yard.

I can see it clearly, the dismembered child – hands, feet, head, the body all in pieces, the blood flowing like a river. Anyone coming near would find themselves up to their ankles in blood.

31

In the middle of all this is a knife. It fell from someone's hand and will never be picked up by the same hand again. And suddenly there's a river carrying it away.

'Have you got room for me where you live?' I ask, sitting the rag-doll Ló beside the real one.

Lóia smiles broadly, ties her scarf around her head with a single knot and nods:

'There's room.'

Yes, perhaps that was where the dreams began, as well as the images that assailed me and that seemed equally like dreams, even if I didn't close my eyes or sleep; perhaps my fear of falling asleep also dates from then, getting out of bed when I was supposed to be taking my afternoon nap, tiptoeing downstairs, and listening at the kitchen door for the familiar sound of saucepans and, halfway down the corridor, the drone of the sewing machine – pfaff, pfaff, pfaff – like the panting of a locomotive.

When it's time for our nap, Orquídea falls asleep at once and isn't afraid at all. Her head lies beside mine on the cotton pillow on which, even in the darkness, you can still make out the flowers, and she breathes slowly, her mouth half-open and her nose pointing up at the ceiling. But I can't sleep. Something threatening is prowling round the house, very close, almost palpable. It almost has a name and a face. But I can't put a name to it, and that, perhaps, is the most frightening part.

I remain vigilant, waiting for some sign. Something might happen, might appear where least expected. I watch with eyes narrowed, like Simba. I look around me without turning my head, I sniff, I feel the air, all my antennae on full alert. I keep my eyes open, even in the dark, observing. I feel that I must be on guard, so as to prevent something from happening, quite what I'm not sure, but something that would split the world in two.

Then the anxiety becomes too much and I get up, pushing Orquídea to one side. She doesn't wake, not even when I clamber over her and roll her to my place in the bed by the wall.

I creep down the stairs on velvet paws. Like Simba. Nothing will betray my presence, I promise myself – not my footsteps, my shadow, my breathing – nothing.

But everything appears to be quiet in the sleeping house. Laureano didn't come home for lunch, Simba is asleep curled up on the rug, Lóia is sitting on the mat in the kitchen, dozing, her head bent forward on her chest, and from behind the other door comes the sound of Amélia's sewing machine.

I take a deep breath and lean back against the wall, my heart racing. Then I slowly climb the stairs again.

I sometimes wake at night and hear voices: Laureano and Amélia are arguing in the sewing-room. But at that hour my body weighs like lead, my legs tremble and I don't have the courage to go downstairs and listen at the door. I stay there huddled among the sheets, unable to make out the words, but understanding the sound of their voices and the tone – Laureano's voice is slow and always the same, as if he were tirelessly repeating the same phrase, and Amélia's is strident, loud, occasionally interrupting his and getting louder still.

The sharp sound of a pair of scissors falling.

Lóia mutters something to herself as she cleans the tiled floor.

'Who are you talking to?' I ask.

'To the ants,' she says, without stopping her scrubbing and without taking her eyes off the floor.

Sometimes, as I say, she would fall asleep for a moment, sitting in the kitchen or in the yard, her head suddenly dropping forward; without waking, she would raise her head and lean it back against the tree or the wall, until it fell forward again. This happened especially in the afternoon, once she had drunk her coffee from the enamel mug. It was as if the coffee made her sleepy. Immediately after her nap, though, she would get up and set to work, more quickly, more lightly, as if she had slept a whole night.

I used to imitate Lóia, although I could never fall asleep straight away like her, my head drooping over my chest, as if it had been hit by a stone. But I learned how to cultivate absent moments. I would sit in the yard, for example, and close my eyes, swaying my body. Or else, with eyes wide open, I would stare at the light. Then the world around me would disappear or move very far away.

Or I would do as she did and talk to the ants. 'Listen to what I have to tell you, ants.'

Well, when you think about it, ants were the best ones to talk to. If you told the birds a secret, they could shout it from the rooftops and spread it throughout the world. With the ants, though, you were safe. And there were so many of them, you never had to look very hard to find them, there was always one close to hand. 'Listen to what I'm going to tell you now, ants.'

Or I would sit down under the tree in the yard and talk to the wind and to the leaves. The tree would wave its branches and I would think: the word tree.

Sometimes, that tree would reappear in my dreams, growing on the bank of a river, its branches reaching up to the sky.

'The water from the Umbelúzi is bewitched,' said Elejana, perched on the edge of the sofa and telling us the story of her wedding for the hundredth time. The heel of one shoe had got caught on some loose threads on the floor and was becoming more tangled up in them each time she moved her foot.

Oblivious, Elejana smiled, blushing and fanning herself in the heat: 'They say that anyone who drinks it is sure to come back,' she said.

Amélia was folding up the dress and placing tissue paper between the bodice and the skirt.

'At least that's what's happened to me,' said Elejana, laughing loudly.

Amélia snorted angrily: 'It would have to be some pretty bad magic to make you come back here.'

Amélia never leaves scissors crossed or open: they could cut off your life, snip the thread, she used to say. She was afraid of spells, of bones sewn into the hem of a dress, cashew seeds slipped down your front, bits of coal left outside doors, buried chicken heads, knives stuck in the ground.

'Not to mention *xipocués*, the spirits of the dead who send disease and death and storms,' said Dona Ismália, gingerly removing the dress she was trying on so as not to prick herself on the pins. Because these things happened. Her cook, for example, went out of the house and found a little pile of salt and, buried further on, the foot of a blue-headed lizard. Ever since then he'd had constant pain in his joints, and his asthma attacks were getting worse and worse. She didn't reckon he was much longer for this world.

And she and Amélia had both sighed: 'Xipamanine market is full of charms and fetishes.'

Once a month, we go to the barber's. Or rather, you go and I go with you. It's always the same barber, in Travessa da Catembe, and he greets us effusively, as if he were waiting for us or as if we were visitors. And even before you've sat down in the chair, with a white cloth around your neck, he's already telling you the latest news: the wrestling or boxing match that took place on the previous evening, or the previous week, at the stadium in Malhangalene, the thunderstorm in Libombos, who's in the lead in the Sul do Save cycle race. Or the shark someone caught near the Yacht Club and how no one had ever seen the like of it before.

While he talks, he snips away at the hairs that appear on the other side of his black comb – small, repetitive, identical movements. You listen, eyes closed, saying, hm, hm, out of politeness. You seem happier when your face is covered in shaving soap and you're excused from having to respond.

He sharpens the razor on a strip of brown leather and tells you about two people who walked all the way from Durban to here. A father and son. It took them two weeks.

From the little stool on which I'm sitting I stare at him in amazement. How did they get here?

He glides the razor carefully across your skin, always avoiding your moustache, which he trimmed earlier on with scissors and comb, and he recites slowly and pleasurably as if he had already moved on to another story: 'Well, they came through Mtubatuba, Gobel, Gaba, and Impamputo. Then Boane and Matola. And before that, of course, they crossed Natal and Swaziland.'

I suddenly feel very hot and go over to the door to see who's passing. Black people – very sensibly it seems to me – always cut their hair outside.

I go back in just as you're getting up from the chair, laughing at whatever the barber happens to be telling you at that moment, shaking his hand cheerily and saying: 'See you soon.'

We step proudly out into the street. Sometimes, we have to go back because we've left behind the little bag of dried fruit and nuts we had bought at the Prodag store for Amélia.

A father and son took two weeks to walk that distance. This piece of news cheers me because two weeks is nothing, and with a little good will we could make the same journey the other way round, from Lourenço Marques to Durban. Or somewhere else. Nothing could be easier, and that way we wouldn't have to spend money on the train. I sigh happily as we turn into Praça Sete de Março and walk across the mosaic designs. Everything is so close, within our grasp. We sit down on a bench, in the shade, facing the Fonte Azul building.

'We'll go to the market on Saturday,' you announce. 'And one of these Sundays, we'll go to Catembe.'

We used to go to Catembe for picnics with Zé Mário and Toninha, Elejana and Margarida Miranda, Gelita, Xana, Agripino, André, Ninito, Jamal, Relito and Bibila. Once, in the rush to get on the boat, we left a picnic basket on the dockside.

That was before Zé Mário bought a second-hand van in Rua do Trabalho and we started going more often to Namaacha, Vila Luísa, Bilene and Ponta Mahone. Or to the Umbelúzi, hunting for partridges, but that was in a smaller group, just you, Zé Mário, Ninito, Jamal and André. And the dogs, of course. I only went with you once, and had to stay close to the van. Afterwards, Bibila and Xana would cook the partridges and we would all eat them at a very jolly Sunday lunch.

Unless, that is, Licínio had an attack of what we called 'phylloxera'. It would come on him suddenly and he'd have to jump in the car and drive off aimlessly down the dirt roads, where, when a car came in the opposite direction, you couldn't see a thing and you had to wind up the windows quickly and cover your mouth with your hands, but even then it would make you cough and splutter and you'd be stuck for ages in the middle of a cloud of red or ochre dust before it settled enough for you to be able to see the road again.

Whenever he had one of these attacks and word got around, we all raced over and jumped in the car, asking each other if anyone had told Ninito, so that he could bring the dog. And as soon as Ninito and the dog were in, we would set off, jolting down the road, with Licínio at the wheel, a fixed expression on his face and not saying a word, but driving faster and faster, while darkness fell. Because that was usually when these attacks happened, and then the attack would pass. At some point, he would suddenly screech to a halt, thump the steering wheel and yell: 'Jeesus!'

That was the signal for us to turn back.

Sometimes we would have a picnic nearer to home, on Polana beach; at first, we used to take the bus, but later, we all travelled in the van, with Zé Mário at the wheel, Bibila sitting between Joana and Ninito's dog, who barked all the way, Xana with Zézé on her knee, and Gelita buried beneath a pile of towels, plastic boxes and bottles of Vimto that couldn't be crammed into the boot.

That was what life was like, and it barely altered with the changing of the seasons – there was Summer and Winter, but no Spring or Autumn. Although we used to say that we got all four seasons in one day: it would be hot one moment, then there would be a downpour heavy enough to stop the traffic, and then, ten minutes later, the air was fresh and the sky was clear again.

It was winter in July and the sun disappeared at five o'clock, you put a blanket on the bed and wore leather shoes, and only tourists went to the beach. January was holiday time because of the heat. Classes started in September.

That was what life was like, you didn't talk to people on the phone, you just turned up at each other's houses – to play cards or to enjoy the cool of the evening after supper, which was served at seven.

Amélia didn't go because she didn't like mixing with the neighbours, and so people rarely visited our house. With time, that became an unspoken agreement. The neighbours always invited her, out of politeness, to picnics and day-trips, but no one ever really expected her to come; out of politeness, too, they pretended to believe her familiar excuses – too much work, feeling unwell, a toothache, a bad back, a migraine.

From time to time, she would tell me not to mix with

certain children – 'Don't play with Tó, Mariquita, Alcino' – simply because she wasn't talking to the mother of one of them. I felt awful, not knowing what to do, and in the days that followed, I would walk past those particular houses, afraid of meeting them or their mothers. I knew what the neighbours said about her: snob, bean-pole, fool. 'If she tried that with me, I'd give her a piece of my mind. Because I reckon . . .' and they would lower their voices if they saw me coming.

On some Sundays, Laureano doesn't want to leave her alone at home and so we stay with her, but we have nothing to say and nothing to do, because all we hear is the buzz of the sewing-machine, and the day seems endless.

The best Sundays were the ones we spent at the house of Jamal and Bibila, when the men had been hunting partridges, Bibila and Xana would be slaving away in the kitchen, and we would all arrive to help; and, really, that took up the whole of Sunday, because, what with cooking, setting the table, stirring the pots, and eating lunch – all interspersed, of course, with a good deal of laughter and horseplay – the day was gone.

No one was worried or anxious about tomorrow, we all surrendered unreservedly to the pleasure of the moment. Bibila would serve lunch with a large spoon, saying: 'This, my friends, is only the beginning, because there's another pot waiting on the stove.' And Relito would say: 'Those partridges don't stand a chance with us around.' And Jamal would ask: 'What do you mean? A chance to be hunted or a chance to be eaten?' And Relito and André would talk about the *sécua* birds and the green doves they had trapped as boys. You would laugh and open another bottle of wine. And no one cared if a glass got broken or someone spilled something on the table cloth.

Lóia would be in high spirits too, laughing a lot, her eyes shining. Her happiness was infectious, and I felt quite different in her company.

Then again, 'sadness' was also a word I heard her use. Of a black man who had died, for example, she might say: 'He got taken by a sadness.'

Sometimes she would sit quite still, thinking. And then she, too, would seem to be plunged in sadness.

'Oh, those blacks and their lies,' says Amélia. 'They say their name's José, João or Joaquim da Silva, then one day, for some reason, it turns out they're called Bulande, Panquene, Maimige, Comenhane or Chinguizo. We know nothing about them. Absolutely nothing. And her over there, her name probably isn't even Lóia at all, or perhaps someone once called her *saloia* – peasant – and she just picked up the last bit of the word and turned it into a fake name to throw back at us.'

'Her real name is Lourdes,' Laureano tells me. 'But Lóia suits her better, it sounds like *ku lóia* – bewitching. It was just a name we invented at random, a pet name. *She* likes it too.'

When Lóia didn't come to us, I would travel in my mind to the place where she lived, even though I didn't know exactly where that was; I would follow her to the edge of the concrete city, enter the *caniço* – the shanty-town – and walk along its sandy paths, in the sparse shade of its few trees, pass through the tangle of tiny buildings and shacks, past the houses with zinc roofs and the straw-thatched huts with adobe walls.

'Lóóóiiaaa,' I would call softly. She would answer, and the sound of her voice would guide me to her door. I would tiptoe into the area where the children were sleeping, find my place and lie down, gently pushing Orquídea to one side to make room.

The mat was cool and, outside, I could hear the noise of the cicadas. I wasn't afraid of the darkness all around me. I was at home. Lóia grabbed fear by the scruff of the neck and sent it far away, into the forest and the jungle. And fear got lost.

The night was as soft as an old sheet, worn smooth by use. Sleep, when it came, would rest the body, like oil massaged into the skin. Tomorrow we would eat almonds and mandioca-and-pumpkin stew. And I was happy and at peace and fell asleep.

And tomorrow Lóia would return and I wouldn't have to feel afraid or hide her purse to stop her leaving. If she didn't come in the morning, I would set off at night to call her – I would seek out where she lived and was sure to find the way – I would go to the edge of the concrete city and keep walking, in the sparse shade of those few trees.

There were other times when it seemed to me that at night there were no real differences. I rediscovered my dark face and lived with Laureano and Lóia in the Black House.

'It's Lóia's fault that my daughter, my own daughter, doesn't love me,' says Amélia. 'Because it's Lóia who tells her these stories, these lies, it's Lóia who puts these ideas in her head.'

Then there was the time Jamal Uamusse and Bibila celebrated their wedding anniversary and went to spend a few days in Johannesburg.

There we all were, on the appointed day, at the station in Praça Mac-Mahon, at two-twenty in the afternoon, excited and noisy and almost as happy as they were, ready to wave them off in the midst of all the heat, the bags, the suitcases, the cries of 'Have a good trip!' and the anxious, last-minute glances around to make sure nothing had been left behind.

'Don't forget the bag with the food in it,' someone says, 'because the train doesn't get in until ten past nine tomorrow morning.'

'It's going to be a long night for the newly weds,' says Relito, and everyone bursts out laughing.

'Yes, ten past nine in the morning, *if* there are no delays,' says Bibila, who is wearing an orange dress and new shoes with a butterfly trim. To be more comfortable on the journey, though, she's brought another pair of flat shoes that she's already worn in, and these she's put in a cloth bag so that they're easier to carry.

Jamal puts his arm around her shoulder and looks as proud as a new bridegroom.

'We'll want to see the photos,' says Xana.

'Well, if you want a photo, take one now,' says Jamal, posing. '*Xithombe*!'

'The reason it takes such a long time is because the train stops so often,' Tito Umbina explains. 'It stops at Pretória, Belfast, Boven, and other places too. By the time you reach Komatipoort, you'll be having breakfast.'

'By car it would only take nine or ten hours. It's about seven hundred kilometres and it's a good road,' says André.

Porters pass, carrying luggage; a few passengers start getting into the carriages, which are upholstered in dark blue velvet with a paler pattern. It's half past two, and the train doesn't leave until two forty-five, but some people are in a hurry to settle in, while others lean out of doors and windows, saying a last few words to those staying behind.

A train pulls in on another platform, belching sooty smoke; there's a deafening whistle and the impatient roar of the engine as it slows, although the wheels take time to stop turning, giving one more turn and still another, and only then do the small doors open and the passengers pour noisily out to meet those waiting for them.

On this platform, people hurry past us to say goodbye to someone or to get on the train. It's two thirty-five, time for a last exchange of hugs, a few final words of advice ('have as much fun as you can, have fun for us as well', 'think of us when you're there'), then they climb aboard along with all their bags and suitcases, which almost block the steps up into the carriage.

And now that they're standing at the window, we hear a bell clang twice. At the far end of the station, a man is furiously tugging on a piece of string, and the clapper bangs loudly against the sides of the bell.

'That means there's only five minutes to go,' you say. Five minutes later, the bell rings again, just once, and the train begins to pull out, and anyone not on board is left behind, but we all think with relief that at least now there's no chance of Jamal and Bibila not catching their train, since they're already on it.

Perhaps because I'm going to miss Jamal and Bibila, I can feel my heart beating very fast as I stand in the middle of that platform with its tall columns that grow gradually smaller and seem to drag us with them to the distant point where they converge. Like iron coconut trees, I think, looking away. Written on the wall in large, framed letters are the words 'Waiting Room' and 'Station Master'. Along either side of the station concourse, doors swing open, huge panelled wooden doors with gleaming brass handles and glass panes bearing a monogram – the letters C, F, L and M intertwined. From the side corridor, tiled in white and blue, come two more figures, running. 'Latecomers,' says someone.

Then the bell rings again, just once, and the train leaves: the air smells of coal and smoke and all the arms are saying goodbye, leaning out of the windows.

We shout 'Have fun' and wave with both hands raised in the air. 'See you when you get back,' we shout, as urgently as if we were watching Jamal and Bibila leave us for good.

It's sunny outside in the square where the buses leave from.

There's the number 4, slowly pulling out. Like the 3 and the 5 it goes to the areas around Polana. And there's the number 1, which goes to Praia or Oásis. And on some days, there's another that takes you from Oásis as far as Ponta do Mar and Costa do Sol. Unless you catch the 12 to the Zoo. And the 13 goes to the part of town where the Blacks live, although Lóia says it doesn't go anywhere near her house.

'Did she like Johannesburg?' I ask, meaning Amélia. Because I know that when you married her, you took her there, on that same train.

'Oh, yes,' you say. 'It's here she doesn't like.'

I know that it's here she doesn't like.

'They may deny it,' says Amélia, 'but the old tertian and quartan fevers are still around. And epidemics too. They say there have been cases of hepatitis and diphtheria in Manhiça and foot-and-mouth disease in Moamba — in both cattle and people. That's what they say anyway. But it's only when a neighbour dies that anyone really believes those diseases are out there, in their own street.'

Preventing contagion was one of her main concerns. To avoid athlete's foot, she used Nixoderm and she never put her bare feet on the floor, not even when she got out of the bath. As if the city might set a trap for her and bite her foot — an animal bite, diseased and foul-smelling. (The city baring its teeth at her small, white, unwary feet in their fine shoes. Tread lightly, run away, keeping close to the walls in the narrowest streets as you flee, like a cornered rat that might, if it's clever, still escape.)

To ward off malaria, she occasionally took Paludrine, even though she was told that taking it like that was counter-productive. And she used to spray the cupboards with Cafum because she was afraid of cockroaches and imagined that she could always hear them whirring about her head.

At night, you could hear the croaking of frogs coming from vacant, marshy plots and areas where the undergrowth was beginning to take hold. It was a familiar, monotonous sound that blended with the silence and was, in a way, part of it. But Amélia complained that it kept her awake. She was afraid of frogs and toads, not to mention snakes, and that was probably why she put up with Simba, because she believed, where there's a cat, there are no snakes.

Not that she liked Simba, which is why she threw cold water over him whenever she caught him sleeping in the yard. She particularly disliked it when Simba jumped onto a marble-topped table underneath the window of the sewing-room and curled up there to sleep on the warm surface, his belly turned towards the sun and his nose resting on his paws.

Amélia watches from inside, but pretends not to see him until he abandons himself to the sun and falls into a deep sleep. She casts apparently distracted glances through the window while she sticks pins in the fabric folded up on her work table, as if she had forgotten all about him. Then, very quietly, she opens the window and tips a jug of cold water over him.

Simba wakes at once and leaps up, shaking himself, then runs away, uttering sad, angry, surprised miaows, while she laughs, a laughter that dies as soon as she sees me, as if she had been caught out. Because she knows that I'll keep watch and make sure Simba doesn't sleep on that table again.

You buy the newspaper and, with it folded up under your arm, we go into a shop to collect some photos. (There they were, Agripino and Relito carrying litre bottles of drink, Bibila in her swimsuit, holding a chicken leg, Ninito with a towel over his shoulders and a mug of beer in each hand, Zézé sitting in front of the group, wearing the newspaper hat that Gelita has put on his head.)

'The second film wasn't put in the camera properly, I'm afraid, and so the pictures didn't come out,' says the assistant, whom we know from other occasions and who is called Evaristo Leão. We burst out laughing because this 'disaster' seems so unimportant, despite what is, for us, the almost prohibitive cost of the photos.

'Oh well, give me two packs of cigarettes instead,' you say. He knows which brand you want and places two packets of Atletas on the counter.

All around are cameras, piled up rolls of film, passepartout frames containing pictures of film stars, signs saying 'Choose Ilford for your photos', framed portraits in the shop window – smiling young women, brides, children. A dog comes in through the door, and Evaristo shoos it out without even pausing as he gives you the change. 'See you again then,' we say.

We leave, carrying the photos, and further on, worn out with walking, we go into a café. It's hot; it's mid-morning, getting on for noon. Two flies buzz around my ice cream, and the bowl wobbles on the small round table with the glass top, on which I'm having difficulty leaning my elbows.

You're finding it hard to get your knees under the table without bumping them on its one leg. But nothing can dampen our spirits, not the blank roll of film, not the table-leg or the too-high top. We're alive, sitting at a tiny table, tired and happy. On the ceiling, the blades of two fans are turning, making a soft humming noise that fits well with the shadowy café.

The Trocado Cauteleiro – the lottery-seller – whom I didn't even notice come in, stops at each table for a chat and to sell the odd lottery ticket – no, no one wants more than one today, or else they've already bought a ticket elsewhere. Perhaps in the Champion lottery or the Lucky Clover Leaf. He leaves, repeating: 'This could be your lucky day.' And for a while afterwards, we can still hear that cry, mingling with the noises from the street.

You spread out your newspaper on the table and slowly take out a cigarette, without even looking at the packet, by touch alone, as if you were blind. I won't say anything, I don't want to interrupt you now. I breathe slowly, I'm connected to the world through my mouth. My breath is a puff, a puff of wind. I share it with the vast horizon around, I am part of it just as it is part of me.

The city surrounds us with its many arms, its many circles. No one can spoil that sense of belonging, of being contained.

We are part of a whole, a living city. Somewhere the ships are passing, coming into port and leaving. On the beach, the children are playing, their swimsuits pale patches of colour in the sunlight. Farther out there will be pleasure boats and, crossing the harbour-bar, steamships, steamers and liners. We would be able to see all this from some high vantage point, from a belvedere, or from a flowering pergola.

I can see nothing, sitting here at this round table in the café, and yet those distant things, like the ships passing, coming and going, form part of this moment, in which everything is contained. I scoop out some ice cream with my spoon and raise it slowly to my mouth. Scarlet cream, redcurrant-flavoured, melting. The taste of summer. Higher up, the acacias will be swaying against the sky. My thoughts are not at all clear, perhaps only a vague approximation. Life fits into a spoonful of ice cream, to be breathed in, devoured.

Everything happens very slowly now, the ships have all the time in the world to leave or enter the port, the children laugh out of pure delight to be playing among the waves. Slowly, slowly. Time is a breath, a puff of wind. It's in no hurry, it lingers, and, for whole moments, seems to have stopped for ever.

Now, though, all around us, the city is in motion again – it grows and multiplies like a kaleidoscope. We will walk down the streets, which we know by heart. In a way, they are inside us, like lines engraved on the palms of our hands. Some are parallel, perpendicular, geometric, while others follow their own course, like the paths carved out by wind or water. The city is a living, breathing body, mine, yours, other people's, the world's; it's an endless intersecting of bodies, caught in the uncountable moments of time, repeated over and over like the waves of the sea. And it's as pointless trying to fix your gaze on it as it is on the waves, because no sooner do they rise up than they've crumpled onto the sand, and our gaze with them.

'They say this summer's going to be hotter than last year,' you tell me, without looking up. 'And next week there will be some amazing reductions at Fabião's.'

It's an orderly city, arranged on regular lines. And yet it isn't domestic or tame or, indeed, tameable. You can't tame the casuarinas, the coconut palms or the jacarandas. Or the bush and the jungle. Although it's true that the jungle had retreated – when Ascendino arrived in the 1930s, the Hotel Polana was being built right in the middle of it. (The very same Ascendino who one day sent you the letter that changed your life. You often told me the story: it had been a spur-of-the-moment decision, made on an impulse, on the very day you received his letter. You left a field half-worked, setting aside your hoe and throwing down your bag. Enough. I'm leaving. Without saying goodbye. And it took you two years to pay back the cost of your third-class ticket.)

The hotel was being built right in the middle of the jungle. And it never occurred to anyone then that it would, for some, become a kind of icon of the city, or of that part of the city, almost a magic word, evoking a whole world: Polana. The city at that time ran parallel to the estuary. There was the older part – the Cidade Velha – the centre, or Baixa, and little else. A few buildings were beginning to go up in Alto Maé and Ponta Vermelha, but there was still a lot to be done.

In the city of Ascendino's memories there were trams sliding along rails, as slow as elephants, and rickshaws with very high wheels riding down the Avenida da República. You had to catch a train to go to the beach and it took ages to get there.

All of this seems to me as remote as Ascendino himself, of whom I only ever saw one photograph – a plump man in shirt, suit and tie and with a white straw hat perched awkwardly on his head, slightly askew, as if he were wearing it for the first time for the purposes of the photo.

He was the owner of the collection of postcards we have of the old city, which seems equally unreal, a paper backdrop, like the ones on film sets.

Only later did the first olive-green buses arrive, which were greeted, you say, as a real sign of progress. But speaking of trains, there was still the one going to Marracuene. According to Ascendino, it looked like a toy, its rickety old wagons labouring along past the back of the cemetery. Schoolboys used to run alongside, racing it, jumping on board and jumping off again by the side of the tracks, pretending to be cowboys in the Wild West – and all around the school lay the jungle.

The letter that changed your life: 'If you're up for it, here I am, and if you're not, stay put, I've enough headaches of my own.'

The time – equally unreal for me – when you were nineteen and first arrived here. You came from a place whose name I can never quite remember, Chão de something or other. In Portugal there were lots of places with curious names, for example, Bom Velho de Baixo, Pé de Cão or Oliveira Santíssima – Kind Old Man at the Bottom of the Hill, Dog Foot, Holy Olive Tree – or Chão do Vento, Chão de Meninos, Chão das Donas – Plain of the Wind, Land of Children, Ladies' Ground.

The first make me laugh, but I like Chão das Donas – the Ladies in question are playing patience, seated on low chairs in a large room and oblivious to the fact that the room is gradually emptying of people. Chão do Vento is a beautiful name and when you say it out loud, the words echo and you can almost hear the wind, which perhaps then blows away the Ladies' chairs, sweeps the ground from under them and leaves them sitting on air. All these thoughts, and many more, are possible, but I have no clear images of Portugal, apart from it being a very small rectangle on the map, on the other side of the world.

There are colourful pictures on the walls of the Café Scala, showing images of Sintra, the Algarve, Lisbon and other places. You can tell it's the Algarve from the almond trees in blossom, and you can tell that it's Lisbon because of the boats and the river.

The city, viewed from Catembe or from the Matola docks, is very similar to Lisbon, you say, when seen from what they call over there 'a Outra Banda' – the other side of the river. A white city at the water's edge. But you don't like talking about 'over there'. The things I hear you say sometimes have a bitter tang to them ('an ill-governed country', 'badly run', 'Lisbon refuses to talk to the Africans').

From Lisbon came photos of Uncle Narciso and my cousins Marivone and Delmira. They were placed on the shelf, where my grandmother's photo ended up as well, after spending a long time on a little table made of chamfuti or pod mahogany. But as the photos multiplied and became too many to fit on the table, Grandma was transferred to the shelf as well. We thought it best to move her, so that she would be among her family. The table, being made of fine wood, provided a more honourable setting, but it's always better to have company.

The table found a new home in the hall, next to the umbrella stand, with a *quinda* or basket on top, containing some dried *maçalas*. We thought the effect very decorative and nodded approvingly. We bought the *quinda* in Xipamanine market, of course, and picked the *maçalas* – whole armfuls of them – when we were on a trip out somewhere. They were round, heavy and glossy, like green oranges. Over time, brown marks appeared on the skin and spread until, eventually, they covered the whole surface and the fruit itself grew ever lighter, but never rotted. When you shook one, you could hear the seeds inside rattle; however, that was only after a year and a half or even two years.

My grandmother, whom I never met and knew only from that one photo, remains a frequent cause of friction between you and Amélia, because you send her money now and then, and Amélia knows this and disapproves.

'Your brother Narciso was her favourite, wasn't he? Not that he bothers with her now. She could drop down dead and rot in a corner for all he cares. Let Narciso send her money, since he was always the golden boy.'

(His mother. At five o'clock, she would shake him awake, drag him out of bed and help him to get dressed or sometimes even put his shoes on for him because he had fallen asleep again, fully clothed and sitting on the edge of the bed.

'Come on, boy, you're never going to earn a living like this,' she would scold him, pouring hot soup into a bowl and filling a mug with wine. 'Come on, it's late.'

He would gulp down the soup and the wine, pull on his cap and his sheepskin jerkin and set off, one hand in his pocket and the other clutching both his lunch pail and the bag holding the work he had brought home with him – the soles that his mother, nodding by the fire, had sewn the previous night, while he was already asleep in bed with his brother.

Off he went to the shoe-factory, a large wooden shack about four kilometres away. At ten years old, he was head of the household and went to work every morning, at least when there was work, because sometimes the boss sent word that he wouldn't be needed for a while. And then there were just the goats to take care of.)

It was a small house, you say, and very cold in winter. Sometimes, before you could wash your face in the morning, you had to break the ice on the water in the jug. And some days, the hail came down the chimney, clattering on the lid of the enamel pot and whistling as it melted on contact with the fire, or else it rapped on the window panes, the stones bigger than grains of rice, about the size of shelled almonds, almost like gravel – which is why you called it *pedraço* – and when the hail beat hard, driven by the wind, you would worry that the glass might break.

When you peered out of the hatch in the front door, the whole road was dotted with white. On the way to school, the boys would pick up handfuls of hailstones that immediately seeped out between their fingers, wet and stiff with cold. The ice on the pond that you broke with a brick or a stone shattered into large brilliant shards through which you could look because they were transparent like glass.

I can't even imagine your father, of whom there was no photo. He was a very remote figure, who had emigrated to Brazil when you were still small, and whom you once saw return, like a ghost. You would have been about seven at the time and were tending the goats.

'I'm your father,' said the man, coming down into the lower field to meet you. But he was a stranger, whom you didn't even remember.

'Where's your mother?' he asked.

'At home,' you said, and felt afraid of the man, afraid of your mother, afraid of what your mother would say to the man, and you wished he had never come or that he would simply go away. But he didn't. He stayed for ten hellish months, during which he never ceased to be a stranger.

Once, he asked: 'Have you counted the goats?'

'No,' you were about to say, 'Basílio counted them.' But you had only got as far as the 'No' when he struck you with a stick made of quince wood. And when, later on, he discovered his mistake, he said nothing and didn't even seem sorry.

You yelled down at him from the roof that you had known how to tend goats long before he ever came and that you'd never lost a single one, and with no help from him either.

That's the part of the story I never tire of hearing, the moment when you start tearing off the roof tiles and hurling them at him, one after the other, refusing to come down and staying up there all day in the rain. Until he goes and fetches a ladder and climbs up after you, armed with belt and stick, not to bring you in from the rain, but because your impudence is driving him crazy. But the roof is wet and slippery, and he moves very slowly and gingerly, because he's afraid of falling and breaking the tiles. Meanwhile, you jump over onto the other side of the roof, light as a cat, and climb down the ladder before he can. No one saw hide nor hair of you for three whole days.

You came home in the end, of course, when you were hungry enough. And the beating you got then was even worse than the first one. But nothing can erase that moment when you stood on the roof and defied him, yelling that you didn't need him to teach you anything – I don't mind how often you tell me that part of the story.

Narciso was born nine months after he left. Unlike you, he bore no resemblance to his father – but this part of the story I will only hear and understand much later, and perhaps you yourself took a very long time to accept it, if you ever did – and it was whispered in the village that the person he most resembled was Ramiro da Feitosa, and that this was your mother's way of avenging herself for all the beatings she suffered during those ten months of hell, and perhaps for the beatings she had suffered during the time of which you remember nothing, before he left for Brazil).

Many years later, he came back again, but you were no longer there. By then, he was a broken old man. He had worked in Rio de Janeiro for thirty years as a tram-driver, and returned to Portugal exactly as he had left, with his pockets empty. 'Clang, clang, clee, one for the company and two for me.' That, they used to say, was the motto of the employees on the Rio trams, but it wasn't true, or not at least in his case.

Your mother and Narciso resisted at first, but finally took him in, because he had no other means of surviving. He still made their lives wretched; he was as evil-tempered as ever and what followed was another period of misery and hell. Then one day, he went up onto the roof to change a broken tile, fell from the eaves and died.

I see that story as being closely connected to the other story, a consequence of it: there's the moment when you're seven years old and you stand on the roof and defy him, and he gives you a beating with stick and belt; then there's the time he climbed up onto the roof to change a tile, fell off and died.

You take out another cigarette and light it without looking, with one flick of the lighter's tiny wheel.

'An ill-governed country,' you say again, 'and badly-run too. The "old man" sits rotting on his perch, surrounded by his fellow chickens, and listens to no one. Not the Africans or the people over there, where they starve in silence.'

I know you're referring to that old man – to Salazar – but I always associate him with your father, who, for me, has no face. When I imagine him attacking you on the path, in the middle of the field, the only thing I can see clearly are the frightened snouts of the goats.

We're sitting in our chairs out on the verandah now, as if we were falling asleep with our eyes open. It's still hot, the house sleeps, the roof sleeps, the yard sleeps. It's the humid part of the summer, there's a different smell about the earth and the wind, somewhere there's the sound of insect wings beating, the buzz of wasps or bees in our ears. The body grows limp with tiredness, then it wakes up, shakes off the general torpor and for a moment is alert, expectant, before sliding back into weariness and sleep.

Yes, we were being assailed and taken over by a kind of drunkenness. Africa was numbing us, slipping inside us like an evil charm. We used to sit on the verandah drinking dark beer (you always let me have a sip of yours) as if the world had ended and we were going to stay there for ever, or perhaps that was precisely what we wanted, to stay there for ever on the verandah, drinking dark beer, and listening to things. Because at the time, if we listened, there was a kind of equilibrium in the world. Each thing glowed with its own light and in its way was perfect.

'I am,' said the tree, shaking its branches, 'the seed opening in the darkness, the water stagnating in the marshes, the jungle sleeping. I am.'

And when you took a deep breath, you breathed in the smell of the jungle, as if it was right there in the yard, very close, as if everything touched and was connected – where the city ended, the shanty-town began, and then the jungle.

The jungle. You plunged into it as if into the sea. And its obsessive presence wrapped about you; the jungle contained everything: reptiles, birds, antelopes, insects, clumps of vegetation and broad desolate areas of scrub. But even those apparently empty areas teemed with life: the cooing of the dove, the hoarse cry of the cururu toad, the crazed song of the cicada. It was there in the tart flesh of fruit, in the sour heart of the *maçala*, in the silent silhouette of mouths, paws, invisible claws, it was there and it touched us and hurt us with the sharp fingers of the knobthorn trees.

We closed our eyes, knowing that we were the prey, and that a force was bearing down on us, like a spell. The wind swept away all thought, and what remained was a single moment, stockstill beneath the burning sun. There was neither past nor future, time left its usual path and measured itself in strange ways, it took on the gigantic proportions of the marula or the mango tree and the tiny dimensions of the bees. Time did not exist, nor did we. In the middle of the void, there were just a few patches of flowers and the perfume of the cashew tree wafting on the wind.

According to Amélia, that place had a debilitating, disorienting effect on certain people, as if someone had put the evil eye on them. You could fall into Africa as if into a well. Africa sapped your energies and sucked you in like quicksand. You could never go back, you were never the same person you were before. If you didn't fight hard enough, didn't stick to your guns, that force would drag you down like an illness – a fatal one. Amélia would say this angrily, looking at us out of the corner of her eye, preferring to struggle with the fading light from the window rather than turn on the electric lamp as she sewed on yet another button or press-stud, another hook and eye. The economical, energetic Amélia, who even did battle with the sun in order to save money, and who, very cleverly, used to make only small stitches in the cloth, never pulling the thread out more than a needle's length at a time and then – only after several such movements, which hardly seemed like movements at all – she would extend her arm and draw out the thread, because she could work more quickly that way and save herself having to repeat the same gesture.

Amélia, who told us over and over that what mattered was earning money, getting on in society and going up in the world. However, there were some people, she would say, fixing us with angry eyes, who were so like the Blacks you would think they'd been born here. Children of the jungle. All that was missing was for them to roll out their mat on the floor of a straw-thatched hut and go to sleep.

That was how life was: there were those who rose and grew more refined and those who went backwards. Laureano and I belonged to the latter group. According to Amélia.

'Too much ambition is bad,' says Lóia, sitting on her heels while she folds the sheets. 'Your heart gets heavy. You become like the *quizumba*, the hyena. He goes this way, then that way. First he wants meat, then he wants fish. He follows this path, then that path. And what do you think happens?'

(One path leads to meat and the other to fish, but the hyena wants meat and fish, and so off he goes, two feet along one path and two feet along another. And the paths grow farther and farther apart, and they say to him, listen, *quizumba*, it's not

56

going to work, don't do it, but he won't listen to anyone and off he goes, two feet along one path and two feet along another, and the paths grow farther and farther apart, and they say to him, *quizumba*, this isn't going to work, bring your feet back to your body and follow one path only, but he won't listen and the paths grow farther and farther apart, and he stretches and stretches until, in the end, his body splits down the middle.)

Weeping with rage, Amélia would accuse Laureano of having no ambition. But *she* did, oh yes, she did. Because life wasn't just about making love and holding hands in the cinema.

'Too much ambition is bad,' says Lóia. 'Ambition is like the *quizumba*. He goes first this way and then that way. Along this path and along that path too.'

'She's like a fire ant or a cow-itch plant. She's like the piri–piri and the knobthorn tree,' says Lóia, still talking about Amélia. At other times, she simply sighs glumly, shaking her head, as if she felt sorry for her: 'She has a *lot* of problems.'

Amélia has pale, greenish eyes that change colour slightly, depending on the light, and she dyes her hair ash-blonde. She rarely goes to the local salon, perhaps because she doesn't like the hairdresser, who uses water warmed up in an enamel coffee pot to rinse her clients' hair, and instead she buys some Palette Colour Shampoo from the corner drugstore and does it herself at home, leaving the foam to take effect for ten minutes each time. She is, of course, pleased with the result – the foreign words on the packet seem to her a guarantee of quality, for she feels an unconditional admiration for other languages, of which she understands only a few words. This admiration extends to the foreigners she sees, especially if they're blond, blue-eyed, six-foot-tall South Africans.

Laureano and I see them too; sometimes they're falling-down drunk or else smashing bottles in bars and restaurants, and we can't detect any superior qualities in them at all; they have huge feet and bear a pathetic resemblance to boiled lobsters, because their skin doesn't tan like ours, it turns bright red and peels, but they don't give up, constantly anointing themselves with all kinds of creams and continuing, with great determination, to roast in the sun. We can't understand why such obviously poor-quality skin should excite such admiration.

What we find particularly irritating, but funny too, is the invasion by those who normally live in more temperate climates – where it even snows sometimes – during what we consider to be our coldest time of year, but which must be the most heat their skin can bear without disintegrating. The 'season', they call it, as they arrive in their hordes and camp out on the beach, almost four thousand people in more than one hundred and fifty caravans and trailers. They have the beach to themselves, which they find doubly pleasing because they don't care to mix with us; they look down on us from their great height as if we were creatures from another planet; they refuse to learn to say anything in our language and, like shipwreck victims, scan the horizon for the life-belt of a sign that says 'English spoken' or 'Afrikaans Gesprek', which they rarely find and which they don't really need because we always try our best to understand them.

The richer visitors are much the same, the only difference being that they don't make a lot of noise and tend not to talk very much; they stay at hotels where children are forbidden and where the coathangers are just at the right height for their arms to reach. But they are no better than the others who crowd into the one area of the beach where hot showers have been installed for their use, and neither class of visitor is worth more than us or than the Blacks; besides, why should anyone be thought to be worth more than anyone else?

It's pointless trying to talk to Amélia about such things, for she clings to the belief that fair-skinned people are at the very top of the racial hierarchy and that dark-skinned Portuguese people are almost at the bottom, just above the Indians and the Blacks. With a little persistence and a lot of hair-dye, she believes that she could be mistaken for a foreigner, which, for her, would be the very highest of achievements.

The idea of placing me in Madame Solange Québec's ballet class, frequented by all the elegant young girls of the city, sprang directly from her hierarchical view of hair-colour and her desire to rise up the social ladder.

Yes, I suppose I'll have to talk about that now, about the despair of pointe shoes and the tortuous positions we had to adopt with our feet, about the embarrassment of ungainly bodies, like plucked birds, moving with the uncertain steps of a goose. I won't come again, I promise myself, scornfully eyeing the fat girls obsessed with their waist measurement, who swear that they would die or cut themselves into little pieces in order to become as light as feathers. I won't come again, I won't wear the white tulle tutu or the black leotard for rehearsals, I won't wear my hair drawn back into a tight bun.

I find the whole thing a torment and an embarrassment: my body sad in that dark, close-fitting leotard, the sweat and tears of trying to perform the splits, the blood on my toenails when I take off my pointe shoes, the teacher's cane tap-tapping on the floor as if it had gone mad: one two three four, one two three four, one two three four.

Madame Québec doesn't want us to have a single hair out of place and insists on making us into wooden or china dolls, into moving parts, like gearwheels. Every exercise is designed to remove the life from the body, to make it malleable and mechanical. I remember the cat who dances when you turn the handle on the box, but at least he was born stuffed and didn't have to be killed first in order to be made to dance.

Madame Carmencita Citron accompanies us on the piano, hammering out a waltz, and she, too, is embalmed and old, with her tortoise-shell spectacles and her smell of mothballs.

I'm leaving, I think again. I'm leaving. Because if I'm going to dance it will be barefoot. And not here, but on the hot earth of the yard, underneath the trees. No one will force my body to submit, no one will kill it. And that isn't the music I want either, I want the real rhythms of this African land.

Because dancing – how could they not see this? – had nothing to do with beauty, age, fatness or thinness or what someone was wearing, nor with the presence or absence of an audience. The dance came to find each person wherever they were, be they male or female, old or young, ugly or pretty, it didn't matter, the dance wanted them anyway, wanted them to dance. And for the dance to enter you, all you had to do was obey. Then your heart became the beat. There was only your heart, which the drum amplified, and your heart was the beating blood of the earth.

But I can't explain because it's very hard to explain and because they would neither hear nor understand. For that reason, I miss half the classes and instead find a bench in the park, in Jardim Vasco da Gama, where I sit and wait for the time to pass before I can go home.

Otherwise, I give in to Amélia's wishes and attend Madame Québec's classes, as a good-will gesture. But that good will cannot conceal my feelings of extreme ill will, and the evening of the yearly show ends badly.

Then again, it started badly too. An old man who resembled a toad appeared at the front of the stage to read out some very lofty and, to me, meaningless phrases. I heard only the pomposity with which they were spoken and the tone of voice, which was part warning, part praise and something almost akin to a threat. As if his words were not to be discussed or understood but merely accepted.

He had a way of pausing before pronouncing the last words in each phrase, which created a false sense of expectation, as in certain homilies when it seems that some new thought is about to be uttered. It immediately became apparent, however, that he had already said precisely the same thing several times but in different words and that all we were expected to do was to listen without really paying attention or simply to pretend that we were listening.

This must be what Laureano calls an official speech, I thought, looking around and wondering if the people who were so proud to be there were the same ones who paraded through the governor's mansion, and if the applause was just the continuation of applause heard elsewhere and those flabby words the same words that had been used on other occasions. I couldn't ask Laureano because he had chosen not to attend. Like me, he disapproved of Madame Québec's dance classes.

Now I almost feel sorry for the toad-like gentleman who continues to speak and who must feel awfully hot. That's why he waves his arms about so much, under the illusion perhaps that he might create a cool breeze if he agitates the air about his head. The people applaud regardless of what he might say. Applauding is all part of it and no one questions this either.

While he speaks, a woman is fanning her face, crossing and uncrossing her legs, staring hard at the zip on the dress of the woman sitting in front. Beside her, another woman is fiddling with her pearl necklace, as if she were saying her rosary. Clearly bored, she distracts herself by tapping lightly on the floor with the toe of her shoe and occasionally sighing. More applause.

Now the show begins. A man comes on and recites a poem, a woman sings a *fado* song, a band performs.

Finally, with great enthusiasm, as if they were the star attraction everyone has been waiting to see, Madame Québec's students are announced. The announcement is followed by a round of applause.

At the piano sits Madame Carmencita Citron, tremulous with anxiety, her bird–like head emerging from her lace collar. She's all dressed in black, the same colour as the piano, and she nods energetically, swaying forwards to emphasise the chords, especially the final chords, whenever the tempo quickens.

We begin to dance, but during the second number, I lose my balance and fall over in the middle of the stage, provoking muffled laughter in the hall and disrupting the routine.

For a moment, it looks as if the performance will stop, the girl spinning round in front of me misses the beat and looks about her, greatly flustered, not knowing what to do next. When I get to my feet, the circle of which I had been a part has vanished, I can't find my place and so disappear behind the curtain, from where Madame Solange is gesticulating wildly and shouting desperately: 'Carry on! Carry on!'

The frightened girls improvise; they have to get to the end somehow. Madame Carmencita Citron is hammering furiously at the piano; some of the steps are performed in the wrong order; and time seems not to pass.

At last, the music stops, the girls smile nervously and bend their knees in a practised curtsey; their families applaud warmly, proudly, as if they had already forgotten the incident, or were savouring the pleasure of knowing that it hadn't happened to their daughters, who are up there on stage being admired and applauded, shining like stars. Whereas the other girl, the daughter of that other woman, almost ruined the whole thing, but, since she's no longer among them and refuses point-blank to take part, she deserves to be where she is, sitting on the floor, grimacing in pain, her foot all bruised and swollen, alone behind the curtain. So says Amélia afterwards, almost incandescent with rage, in the taxi on the way home.

But now no one passes comment, apart from the usual polite enquiries; the other girls crowd round her, hurriedly asking: 'Does it hurt very much?' before rushing off to don their veils in order to perform 'In a Persian market'.

Madame Citron advises me to put my foot up on a chair, with a bag of ice on it, but there is no ice and no one bothers to go and find any. Madame Québec quickly invents some new steps to compensate for my absence and explains it twice, so that the girls will understand.

In the taxi, Amélia is furious, partly because she's paid for the whole term in advance. But I swear that I will not go back.

'Never,' I say, 'I'd rather die.'

Months later, I still assure her that my foot hurts when I walk on it, pretend that I can't bear to put it down on the ground for any length of time, and make a point of limping whenever I think Amélia is looking at me. In the end, she gives in.

And I continue to dance barefoot, clapping my hands, beneath the trees in the yard.

Now is perhaps also the moment to talk about the clothes that Amélia made me wear whenever I went out with you: patent leather shoes, white socks and a hair ribbon the same colour as my dress.

She wants me to look exactly like the girls in the fashion plates, but I feel like a performing dog. The first thing I do once I'm out in the street is to remove the ribbon and give my hair a good shake. And when we take our seats on the bus, I stuff the socks in my pocket and kick off my shoes. (I know what she would say: 'Anyone seeing you would think you came from the shanty town.') I rest my bare feet on the back of the seat in front and really stretch.

Amélia always tells me off afterwards because I've creased my dress or spilled ice cream down it. I hate those dresses made of tobralco or silk, I hate boleros and lace blouses, and percale skirts that don't let me move freely and make me feel like a mannequin, all frills and ribbons, a celluloid doll, with ringlets and glass eyes, standing in the window, as dead as she is. I look at her with my living eyes and swear: 'I don't come from you, I come from Lóia. Tomorrow, I'm going to wear a *capulana*, like Orquídea.'

But I don't want to think about Amélia. ('Go to the cinema? This evening? No, I couldn't possibly. There's that dress of Elejana's to finish. Besides, I've got the most dreadful headache.')

We go to the Scala or the Varietà (the latter hadn't yet been demolished, that only happened later, in 1967). Or perhaps to the Gil Vicente in Avenida Aguiar (which, at the time, still hadn't been renamed Dom Luís) – because the Gil Vicente is also close to the places we usually visit in the area between Avenida da República, Avenida 18 de Maio and the harbour.

The Manuel Rodrigues, on the other hand, is further up, in Avenida 24 de Julho. We went past there yesterday by chance and read the posters: *Vile Treachery*, *Pleasure and Violence*, *The Chorus Girl*, *Bed of Thorns*, *Beautiful Liar*. We never pass a cinema without looking to see what's on today or what they'll be showing next or on Sunday, when there's usually a double bill, and what the new film will be on Tuesday. We stand and stare at the bright colours, the garish contrasts, they seem to draw us towards them when we walk past, and even in a car, driving fast, it's impossible to look away without first reading what they say.

Virginia's Secret – aimed at the discerning film-goer – was being shown yesterday at the Manuel Rodrigues, and was to be followed by *The Spy with Two Faces*, a nerve-jangling thriller, an unforgettable film that will linger in the mind, one moment moving you to tears, the next making you laugh out loud.

Sometimes, the names of the films you took me to see suddenly surface in my memory, or titles only glimpsed on posters or others I perhaps invented. I can't always tell the difference and I ask you so as to test myself out: 'Do you remember *Tarzan the Magnificent*? *Norman on Stage*? *Murder in*

Machava? *A Dollar's Worth of Fear*? (And where did I read titles like these: *Lips that Burn* and *Flying to the Stars*?)

It's still early, but there's already a long queue outside the box office of the Scala. We take our place behind everyone else, slightly worried that we might not get a seat. It wouldn't be the first time that tickets have sold out before we reach the head of the queue. This is usually because someone turns up late, checks to see if he knows anyone near the front, and then goes up to them and asks the friend or acquaintance to buy five or even ten extra tickets for him and his whole family – so it's hardly surprising that the tickets sell out fast and that the queue doesn't seem to move.

I shift impatiently from one foot to the other, and end up going to have a look at the entrance to the cinema while you wait in front of the people who have, almost instantaneously, formed a line behind you. I walk past painted figures, half-naked men leaping from skyscrapers with a woman in their arms and a pistol at their waist, planes plummeting earthwards, forests on fire, the heads of lions, which, seen from the street, seem gigantic. *The Object of Desire*, thrilling, bold, tense, taut, a film – here another poster, pasted on top, interrupts my reading – I walk round to the other side and, with some difficulty, decipher the rest of the sentence on another smaller poster inside the glass showcase – a film full of suspense and unexpected twists and turns.

Reading the posters is almost as good as seeing or imagining the film – I walk to and fro, letting the words spin around inside my head. Some films frighten me, others attract me even though they're frightening; they make my heart beat faster, my chest tighten, and I start to sweat despite the air-conditioning to be found in all the cinemas, with the exception of the Varietà. But this, I notice, is not the film being shown today, nor this one, *Cruel Power* – gripping and original. Finally, in the middle of all the other advertisements, I find one that says: Today, matinee at 15.00, evening showing at

20.30. *The Paths of Sunset*. One of the most beautiful films ever made – not to be missed. Enchanting. Unmissable. Absolutely divine. The film of the year. The poster shows a red plain on which scenes of war are being played out, with bombs exploding, and a man and a woman, both very tall, with their backs to us, who appear to be walking towards a tiny house in flames on the horizon.

I return to your side, feeling very excited. I imagine that actors must lead extraordinary lives and be really amazing people. Everyone all over the world knows their names, the newspapers never tire of talking about them, the cinemas plaster their faces onto those huge sheets of paper. And on the posters, in giant letters, are words such as: bold, tense, taut. A remarkable, thrilling, suspenseful movie.

You, meanwhile, have left your place in the queue and have come to look for me. 'It's not worth waiting,' you say. 'It's sold out.'

But we might still be in time for the film at the Varietà. We hurry off to Rua Araújo, home to the Aquário dance hall, which bears on its sign a fish with a single brilliant dorsal fin, arching its body as it leaps. Above the fish is the round belly of a bowl, to which the fish is attached by the air bubbles coming out of its mouth. It seems very pleased to have leapt out of the water, and maybe the huge question mark emerging from the bowl is a comment on the odd fact that the fish appears to be able to breathe out of water and still blow bubbles.

There's a lot of traffic here, an almost constant flow, with cars parked all along the pavements.

Right next to the Aquário is the Varietà, which looks rather old and weary, despite all its many adornments – the ornate little balcony up above, the two columns supporting the arcade at the entrance, the triangular pediment bearing the name of the cinema. Above the horizontal lines of the façade are semicircular skylights that open inwards and, below them, large posters advertising the films. We don't have time to read them now; we hurriedly search for what's on today: *Souls in Conflict*, this latest production from Metro Goldwyn Mayer – a superb, brilliant, passionate drama, totally absorbing. We exchange a brief look, but we've already decided, with no need for words: 'Let's go in.'

In July the days were shorter. By five o'clock – not long after we'd had our afternoon nap – it was almost night. If we lingered a moment longer in the yard, underneath the jacaranda, the sky would suddenly grow dark.

It was at about this time that the word 'promotion' began to be mentioned. At first, it was as if the word hadn't even been spoken, it passed by us so lightly, barely brushing our ears, instantly forgotten. Then it became more insistent, like rain falling and falling, and in time, it filled the whole house, as if it were the only word that mattered.

It was like a magic formula: promotion at work.

Amélia seemed happy and went to John Orr's to buy a marshmallow pink handbag.

School started in September. All of a sudden, we were back in the classroom and the teacher was talking about 'thought paths', meaning: radio and telegraphic communications. But 'thought paths' was a far more beautiful way of putting it and certainly more exact. Because nothing is as rapid as thought, nothing travels so far or so instantaneously over the seas to the other side of the world.

Outside, through the white slats of the shutters, the trees look as if they had been drawn with a ruler, forming very fine parallel lines. In one corner – I can see it from here – grows a mafurra tree.

The teacher is plump and ageless, and has the wistful air of an old-fashioned rag doll. Her very large bosom begins almost immediately under her chin, and the skin on her neck is flabby and flaccid. She's always repeating the same things and she wears her hair in a kind of fat roll at the back of her neck, secured on either side with a comb. Every now and then, she adjusts the other pins keeping her hair in place, making sure that the pointed end is facing inwards. They may be called invisible hair pins, but they're easy enough to spot. They drop onto the floor sometimes or around her chair.

Generally speaking, she doesn't spend much time sitting down, she patrols between the desks and sometimes she looks almost worried. While she's standing in the aisle with her back to us, Roberto takes a pencil out of his pocket and we play noughts and crosses. Occasionally, we have to stop halfway through, until she turns her back on us again. We keep a sharp eye on the movements of her dark blue dress with the white polka dots and on her gold earrings in the form of a heart.

'I am, you are, we are,' says Dona Eulália, and we chorus it back to her, swaying backwards and forwards at our desks, and we write in our exercise books a very sloping F for February and for Fanisse, a J for Jussa, an M for Margarida and Miranda, a Y for Yasmin and a G for Gita.

Writing is difficult because it's awkward holding the pencil, your fingers soon get dirty and smudge the paper, the corners of your exercise book get bent and you have to wet your index finger with spit to turn the pages, and then, if you lose your rubber, you have to try and erase any mistakes with your hands.

An air of weariness hangs over us, we sigh a great deal, mouths half-open, tongues sticking out, tips turned upwards, and we frown as we concentrate on tracing the shapes of the L and the P and the I. Is it Elejana or Ilejana? Margarida wants to know because she's Elejana's daughter. Margarida Miranda, the one in the frilly blouse.

Dona Eulália sits down again on her chair and cools herself with a Chinese fan made of painted paper. She calls the fan a *ventarola*. And she calls the multiplication tables 'houses': the house of four, the house of five.

'Infulene, Munhuana, Alto Maé,' says Yasmin, because Dona Eulália has asked a question. And Luatina, whom we call Titita, adds slightly hesitantly, 'Lhanguene, Malanga.' And Joana says: 'Maxaquene.' And then no one says anything.

And we scuff our feet on the floor impatiently, or do so with just one foot and bend the other leg, bringing it up to the level of the desk lid, then sit on the heel, and not one of us can remember how much seven times eight is.

Xandinha arrives late and says that two houses have been burned down. In Rua do Trabalho. Burned right down. Near where I live. When? At ten. Or eleven. No, it was early in the morning. Was anyone killed? I don't know. No, apparently not. No one died. Everyone ran to help. The firemen came. The neighbours too. Two houses. Burned down.

Dona Eulália sighs and checks our exercise books, moistening her finger with saliva to turn the pages. We notice that she has one white hair on the top of her head and that when she bends over us, she smells of face powder, sweat and mothballs.

We're standing round her desk, on which there sits a blotter that looks like a boat. It has a rounded bottom and rocks back and forth until it stops still beside the glass inkwell with its two containers of ink, one blue, one red.

We recite the lesson together, but not all of us know how to read and haven't even opened the book at the same page. We answer by rote, without looking at the words: *gi-ras-sol*, *rí-ci-no*, *ma-fur-ra* – sunflower, castor-oil plant, mafurra.

The sound of breathing. Ours. The smell of children. We are sweating with the heat and the effort – not moving is the most difficult thing of all.

Xavier stares at the blackboard, his face grown long with concentration. Jussa scratches his head and looks and looks, but can't find the answer, then suddenly laughs out loud and drops a shoe. Joana's hair falls over her eyes, she pushes it back with her hand. Yasmin's ponytail flicks her in the face when

Yasmin abruptly bends down to pick up an escaping pencil. A ruler falls.

Roberto has a frog in his pocket; the other day he had a cricket. Titita has a dog that always waits for her at the end of the road. Assa must be older than us because she's much taller and has lost one of her front teeth.

I learn to write my name in the exercise book: Zita Marcelino Capítulo, Zita being my real name and Gita my nickname.

And when we leave the classroom, Fanisse presses her nose to my face and pretends to vomit: 'You smell so bad. Like a corpse,' she says. 'Like a white person. All white people smell like corpses.'

And one day I ask Assa during playtime: 'Have you ever seen any magic?'

She laughs and opens her eyes very wide. She has, oh yes. 'When I was little,' she says, laughing still more and saying:

'The boys they came at night and rubbed a herb on the handle of a hoe, then they clap their hands, and we girls we stood around looking, clapping like them and singing. And then the handle of the hoe rose up without no one touching it.'

'What did you sing?' I ask.

She claps and recites:

'Npiné oiwe, npiné oiwe,
Npiné oiwe, npiné oiwe,
Npiné lamuca npiné
Vuca, vuca, vuca!'

I sing along with her, clapping my hands, *npiné oiwe, npiné oiwe*, and Assa, almost choking with laughter, says again: '*Vuca, vuca, vuca!*'

Zita Marcelino Capítulo – that's my name, the one I inherited from you, Laureano Capítulo. That's the name they'll say at work, perhaps over the phone, perhaps over the loudspeaker, when they summon you up to the office, when you get your promotion.

We might buy a van like Zé Mário's. We could go on a trip, to see waterfalls, herds of elephant, Lake Niassa, Ilha de Moçambique. We might go on a plane. Or on a big game safari, once you've bought that rifle you're always telling me about, I can't remember the make, it was a foreign word I found hard to pronounce.

We're looking at the windows of the shops in Rua Consiglieri Pedroso and at the Indian jewellers in Avenida General Machado, and you're thinking out loud, as if you were talking to yourself, about what you'll be able to buy Amélia. A ring, a brooch, a string of real pearls, to replace the ones made of majolica that you gave her when you were engaged. Or perhaps a fur stole to wear in winter. Unless she'd prefer a pair of snakeskin shoes with matching purse.

We go into the shops, but neither of us has much experience of shopping, because we don't usually buy much. We are struck dumb with amazement by the profusion of things on sale and by the efficiency of the assistants, who show us first one thing then another, each more expensive than the last. We're overcome by anxiety, but fortunately, there's still time, your promotion won't be until the end of the year. We don't have to decide now, we explain with a nervous laugh, we're just looking.

'But you do need a jacket,' I say. A white linen jacket, made to measure. I always thought you should have one.

And that is how we find ourselves standing outside a tailor's shop in Rua da Gávea. The entrance is very dark and as soon as we go through the door we have to climb some very steep stairs. It's clear that one part of the building is shop and the other part someone's home. We hear hurried footsteps going up other stairs that we can't see, but that clearly lead further into the house. I know that a very confusing architecture often lies behind these façades; some of the houses are connected inside and merge into one, so that you can't really tell where they begin or end; when casting a furtive eye through the half-open door of one of those buildings in Gávea, you sense a labyrinth of corridors, stairs, rooms, dusty windows, the occasional inner balcony that gives onto a room down below. But all of this is safe from prying eyes, and the women too are protected in those deep, dark interiors.

Behind the wall, a voice calls out a name I can't quite hear, a child answers, another child yells, while yet another, or perhaps the same one, jumps up and down on the floorboards. I wonder if the child has a skipping rope or if he or she is playing with a ball, alone or with someone else. I listen closely for a moment to see if the movement is regular or intermittent. I try to tell the voices apart. Now, though, it's a woman saying something in an angry tone; a child is crying, a very small child, possibly a babe in arms; the woman is murmuring something inaudible, to soothe the child, then she speaks more loudly to the other children, who appear to stop what they're doing only to start up again at once.

'Lakshmi,' shouts the tailor, opening the door, his tape measure hanging round his neck, 'where's the order book?' He seems annoyed, because he had looked for the book on the table where it usually was, but couldn't find it.

A girl wearing a sari, and with a red mark between her eyebrows, immediately appears with the book, as if she had been listening at the door. She smiles faintly and disappears again on noiseless feet and with a tinkle of bracelets. The man stands up and strokes his chin; he looks thinner than he did a moment ago.

'Is she your daughter?' you ask. He shakes his head, no, he only married three years ago, he has one small son and is expecting another. 'She's carrying,' he adds, meaning that she's pregnant.

It's clearly a very large family, perhaps more than one, living all together, and to judge by the noise coming through the thin wall that separates the shop from the rest of the house, it must be fairly chaotic in there. And yet everything seems extremely well organised: the girl who appeared as soon as she was called, with her pencil sharpened, to write on the open page of the diary; her instantaneous appearance and disappearance, as if she were playing a part that had been given to her or had fallen to her by chance. Life, I imagine, must be a struggle to keep chaos at bay in the small world between those walls, and still more of one to survive in the world outside the house. They are also bound perhaps by a common religion, as well as by family ties.

Despite the tiny space and the minor incident with the order book, the shop is perfectly tidy: four fashion plates have been arranged on a low table, next to a glass vase filled with dried flowers. Underneath the leather armchair on which I'm sitting is a dark red Indian rug, and on the walls, which they clearly painted themselves, because here and there the paint has been applied too thinly, are pictures of suits and jackets cut from magazines.

The man listens very gravely to what you have to say, fixing you with his large eyes. He takes your measurements twice, to be sure there is no mistake, writes them on an empty page in his book, where, at the top, he has made a note of your name and address. He assesses the quality of the cloth by rubbing it between thumb and forefinger. 'Excellent,' he says again. Despite his dark complexion, his skin looks rather pale.

'At your service, sir,' he says by way of farewell, leading us to the door and smiling shyly. 'I look forward to enjoying your custom in the future.'

We go out into the street again and walk down the packed, buzzing, scurrying streets, full of smells and bodies and the stubborn, inexhaustible life of every day, and crammed, too, with people of many different races. A chance stroll is all it takes to spot the different skin-tones of the passers-by. Just as a drop of white paint mixed in with some black will lighten it and another drop lighten it still more, to create a kind of matte colour, so, among Indians, dark-skinned Whites and Mulattos, there was a great variety of tones; just as, the other way around, a drop of Negro blood darkened pale skin and a second drop made it darker still, producing a skin colour that was sometimes contradicted by the accompanying straight hair and pale eyes.

You could find every possible combination there, or so at least you were led to suspect – White and Black, Indian and White, Indian and Black or Mulatto, Black and Chinese, Indian and Chinese, and every other possible blend; because people didn't live separately somewhere else, bodies met and mingled, discovered secret affinities, hidden complicities. Or were attracted to each other by their evident differences, because that did happen; you only had to ask visiting South Africans, those who dared to admit it, those who found here, in Rua Araújo, something that was punishable by imprisonment in their own country, namely, sex with the other, with someone of another race.

'Oh, my friends,' said Jamal and Bibila when they returned from Johannesburg, 'you might think you know what it's like, but it's really beyond imagination, you have to see it with your own eyes.' It wasn't simply that one part of the city was for Whites and another for Blacks, with hotels and restaurants for Whites, and hotels and restaurants for Blacks, buses for Whites and buses for Blacks, no, the law of separation was applied even to the smallest things.

For example, the benches in the parks and in the streets bore notices saying 'Whites' and 'Non-Whites'; in the post offices there were counters selling stamps for Whites and other identical counters selling the same stamps, but bearing the sign 'Non-Whites', as if the stamps were not the same, or the postcards or the letters, or the money with which they were bought.

Whites lived in fear of touching or even getting close to Blacks, as if Black people had leprosy or as if the colour of their skin were an illness. There were different drinking fountains for Whites and Blacks, even different Coca-cola machines. Everything was separate, a line had been drawn between them, an invisible wall so obvious that you were constantly bumping up against it with body and eyes.

And if, for example, Whites and Blacks had to walk along the same pavement, the Blacks had to step off to make way for the Whites.

I burst out laughing because such foolishness seems so absurd it's laughable. 'They're *so* stupid,' I say to you, hopping my way across Praça Sete de Março. 'Don't you think they're just unbelievably stupid?'

We walk down the streets to the bottom, where we enter the docks and walk along the quay.

This was always my very favourite walk. Your gaze got lost among the forest of ships, the tall silhouettes of derricks and cranes, the tracks that ran for miles along the ground, the way the anchored boats bobbed and swayed, their black hulls appearing and disappearing with the movement of the waves. And then there was the smell – not even a very pleasant one, but intense and familiar, a smell of oil, water and mud – as well as the names and acronyms that we remembered from having heard them so often, *Robin*, *Farrel*, *Gold Star*, *Lykes*, *South African*, *Deutsche*, *Cotts* and others.

This is a port-city, a city-quay, and it's here, facing the broad estuary, that its heart beats fastest.

When you first came to live here, the day that a ship was due into port was called 'Steamship Day'. The whole city emptied and everyone raced down to the docks, even people who weren't expecting anyone rushed to see the ship and would sometimes spend two hours standing in the sun. Later on, it was party time, with the sailors filling the streets and the bars, the shops staying open all night; even now it's a bit like that, although no one would race down to the docks simply to see a ship come in. Nevertheless, the ships are part of our life, they depart and arrive, bring things and people and carry them away, and we can measure the time by their comings and goings because they're as regular and dependable as the seasons of the year, the months, the tides and the phases of the moon.

You tell me that some ships take on cargo bound for Durban, Cape Town, Lagos, Port Harcourt, Victoria, Takoradi, Abidjan, Monrovia and Freetown, and others sail to Bremen, Hamburg and Antwerp, to Trieste or the Gulf of Mexico, to India, Vancouver, New York, Sydney, Mauritius and other places. And there is a rhythm in that movement of people, in those exchanges of cargo being transhipped and loaded, and somewhere deep inside us is the certainty that we are connected to all those other places, to India and to Europe, to Japan and to Australia, and to the Americas, a certainty that the whole world passes through our city.

We find some crates in the shade and sit down. The ships change, they come and go, they never stay, and yet it's perfectly possible – merely by dint of habit – to establish some order in that tangle of shipping lines. (Yes, we want to understand what happens around us, to organise the world, which is why we sharpen our minds and laugh at our discoveries, because thinking is a pleasure: we link one thing with another and then another and finally a pattern emerges. It's probably the same with everything, the universe must be full of clues, like signs in the jungle.) For example, the ships on the Robin Line, which is owned by Cotts, and that sail between Africa and North America, are usually called *Robin* something or other, *Robin Mowbray*, *Robin Locksley*, whereas those with the word '*African*' in their name – *African Moon*, *African Comet*, *African Mercury* – belong to the Farrell Line owned by Rennie, and they, too, shuttle between the United States and Africa; the CNN ships have Portuguese names, of course, which makes it easier for us, and they're called *Príncipe Perfeito* or some such thing, while those with the word 'Maru' in the name are Japanese, although they are also often under charter to Cotts (the *Eiken Maru* is one example).

Sometimes, we test each other on the nationality of the ships in harbour or ones that we remember having seen before, either here or in the Matola docks, and whoever gets it right or wrong gains or loses a point. Some are easy; for instance, the *Ugolino Vivaldi* and the *Sebastiano Caboto* are obviously Italian (especially when you say the name out loud in that sing–song fashion), and the *Krugerland* is, of course, German, but which of us remembers that the *Virtala* is Swedish or the *Shavit* Israeli? It's easy to make a mistake.

And how are you supposed to know where the *Lommaren* or the *Nuddea* are from? And the *Mormac Penn*? And how can you tell if the *Walvis Bay* is British or American? And then there's the *Braemer Castle*, which seems to have a name that is half–German, half–English? We could, of course, tell by the flags, if we knew them, but even so they have to be close enough for us to make out the designs and the colours.

To the right of the ship flying the Greek flag is a smaller boat on which a man is washing down the deck with a broom and soapy water. Next to his bucket is a small black box, which is probably a transistor radio because we can hear, from where we're sitting, the faint sound of a voice singing in the distance.

In the ship immediately in front of us, the head of a goat unexpectedly appears at a porthole, very close to where a sailor is painting some steps, just below one of the funnels. Two men throw down a plank and walk along it onto the quay. They notice us laughing at the goat's head and they laugh too.

'Would you like to come on board?' they ask, as if they were new arrivals offering their house to the curious eyes of the neighbours. Up above, the sailor continues patiently painting. A puff of white smoke emerges from the funnel.

'Yes, please,' we say at once, because we are always ready to embark on an adventure. A black man holds out his hand to us from the other side of the wobbly plank, and helps us jump on board. Another man is pegging out clothes on a piece of string hung between two hooks, and drops of water drip very slowly onto the scrubbed wooden deck.

A ship is like a house, I realise. A house that moves and travels from place to place. There is even the smell of a kitchen, which one reaches by going down some very steep steps, the last flight of which is made of metal. The oven is on and two bare-chested men are chopping vegetables and throwing the resulting debris into a bowl full of fish bones, onion skins and coffee grounds.

'Have a drink,' says one of the cooks, placing some beer on another table where three men are already sitting. We sit down and drink; it's very hot, and a combination of the beer and the movement of the boat is making me dizzy, but I wouldn't leave for anything in the world because everything that happens from now on is part of the wave into which I've just plunged. The sailor who was painting the steps has joined us, and we shuffle our chairs closer together to make room for him, laughing and speaking rather too loudly.

Two large shells serve as ashtrays; everyone smokes, including you, and a thickening cloud grows around us. I drink more beer and the whole ship seems to be spinning; I grip the edge of the table hard and feel that everything is possible, that the ship could, with us on board, set sail, and tomorrow we'd find ourselves in Singapore. Everything is possible, everything, I think, as the ship sways, and suddenly the sight of a goat's head peering out of a porthole seems a very minor miracle indeed.

When we finally get home, we notice that your white linen jacket, which we had picked up earlier in Rua da Gávea – after two further fittings carried out meticulously and in silence – has got paint on one side, and right at the front too, where it's most visible. You must have leaned against the banister, newly painted in black. 'I obviously failed to see the sign saying "Wet Paint",' you say wryly.

I'm grimy with oil as well, and my dress probably looks like an old rag; my hands are black, I've lost my hair ribbon, but we don't care, we're radiantly happy, as if there were some sort of indissoluble agreement between us and the world.

We don't even get annoyed when Amélia rages at us because of the state of my dress or your jacket ('People who don't know how to wear clothes should live in the chicken run'), we listen but don't hear, we just let her talk. A long time will pass, possibly weeks, before she says: 'I'll see if I can undo the front and move the stained part round so that it's in the seam. But only when I've got time, mind. I'm not promising.' Yes, we let her talk and meanwhile eat our pineapple in brandy and sugar.

When I'm at a loose end, I turn on the globe that we bought in Minerva Central, and which serves both as a lamp and a map of the world, and I play at ships on my own, tracing their routes with my finger.

I sometimes imagine what those cities must be like. Travellers would arrive in Singapore at daybreak and see the silhouettes of temples on the skyline, whereas they would always arrive at the tired old European ports at night. Europe didn't appeal to me much; according to you, the sky there was grey and the air heavy and dark. The winters were harsh too, and I didn't like the winter. Europe had the same mechanical heart that beat in New York, but New York was higher up and colder, like an iron tower with its feet in concrete. On the other hand, I felt sure that Africa was the most beautiful continent in the world.

Apart from when we bought the globe, I can't remember many other shopping trips to Minerva Central. You were never one for buying magazines or books, but records were another matter, and you never missed a sale at Grundig's. You would come home looking very mysterious and bearing a square package wrapped in paper. And if you came home at lunch-time, I would have to wait for the rest of the day. I would unwrap the package, take the record out of its sleeve, turn it this way and that, studying its two black sides, then I would place it on the turntable, but without actually playing it, and finally, I would put it back in its sleeve until you returned. And it was only later that evening that we could sit down on the floor and listen, like listening to stories after sunset, because the music told stories too: there was a constant connecting thread, from which phrases rose up and walked onto the stage, like characters in a play. Extraordinarily free phrases, almost obsessive some-times, that seemed to have ended, but always came back, exactly as they had first appeared or else concealed inside variations as if behind a mask. Or split into fragments, splintered.

Those phrases, I felt – my heart beating faster – had to do with life, with our life because they, too, had their regular routines, but also left room for improvisation, even for the impossible. And sometimes, especially during those crazy saxophone solos, they left room for disaster too.

'Jazz,' you say. I know it's jazz. There used to be jazz nights at the Penguin Club in Rua Araújo, where you knew all the musicians in the group, who played saxophone, piano, electric guitar and drums.

But that, I think, was a long time ago, before Amélia and before me.

Now we were in December, and we listened to jazz each night and thought that soon everything would change because, at

the end of the year, you would be promoted to a better position. There were two candidates, and you had been in the
company the longest. Life had seemed to revolve around that
word 'promotion' ever since July. You would say for example:
'When I get promoted' or 'Once I've been promoted'.

But the end of the year arrived, and you weren't promoted.
They merely gave you a small salary increase for being a loyal
and faithful employee, as they told you when they summoned
you to the office at the end of the day.

You couldn't think of anything to say and left.

Outside, it had begun to rain hard.

Later on, the rain grew heavier still, the wind got up and a
storm broke over the city, causing widespread damage, especially in the centre, in the Baixa. The following day, we
learned that the Avenida da República had been flooded
because the drains hadn't been able to cope and because, to
make matters worse, it was high tide.

Piles of sand had accumulated in various places; buses
and cars got trapped in floods and landslides, which had to
be removed by bulldozers. One lane of the Avenida Marginal
was blocked, and next to the Dragão de Ouro, some street-
lamps had fallen over, their foundations washed away by
the rain.

You arrived home in the middle of the storm. We were
waiting for you, with the table laid for supper.

Only over dessert did you tell us what had happened at
work. You stammered slightly.

For a second, all we could hear was the thunder outside and
the rain beating against the windows.

Finally, Amélia sank back in her chair, sobbing loudly, then
she got up and burst out laughing.

'So you reckon he's a rabbit, do you?' she said, addressing
me, but pointing at you. 'Rabbits are clever, but he's not. I'd
say he's more like a marmot, yes, that's what he is, a marmot,

a stupid African marmot with no claws and no guts. Good enough to be eaten, but not for anything else.'

'A loyal and faithful employee,' she said, laughing shrilly and pacing up and down the room. 'A loyal and faithful employee.'

Her voice was becoming ever more strident, threatening at any moment to crack.

' "Faithful" is what you call a dog,' she screamed at last, thumping the table with her fists.

A marmot, a stupid marmot. The words whirled around in the air, the way bats perform blind somersaults as they advance through the darkness, avoiding the light. I hear the words cutting the air, like stones that drop inside us as if into a well. A marmot, a stupid African marmot.

Once spoken, words never disappear, they can't be swallowed by the mouth that uttered them. They're transformed into stone, take on a life and direction of their own. They never turn back.

The lie has, I feel, just entered the world, has grown as high as the sky and will never return to the mouth that spoke it. A lie is like a misfortune, which, at first, kept its distance from people and did them no harm, then it reached the trees, leaving them maimed, twisted and moaning in the wind, bent towards the earth rather than reaching skywards, mad trees, more dead than alive, unable to tell day from night, sun from rain. Then that same misfortune left the jungle and entered the town and crippled the people there, just as it had the trees.

A lie is like a misfortune, those it touches are never the same again. I know that now. I know that lightning can strike at any time and leave the world shattered.

'I wasn't even aware of having slept,' I think as I lie between the sheets the next morning, my body aching and my head heavy. My head is throbbing and, when I look in the mirror, I see that my eyes are puffy.

I go downstairs to the kitchen. Simba follows, then, halfway down the corridor, overtakes me and slips through the open door of the sewing room. Amélia isn't there, I notice as I pass. I go into the room too, in pursuit of Simba, and I'm just about to leave again with him in my arms, when I turn and see Laureano's jacket on the table. Next to the scissors. In pieces. From close to, the scissors look larger: the two sharp metallic blades parted, forming a long voracious mouth. I imagine Amélia cutting, slashing. The jacket in tatters on the table: the collar thrown to one side, like a puppet's tie, the long, long sleeves spread out, unstitched, the lining hanging out of the pockets like the entrails of some slaughtered animal. (And all of this for one small paint stain?)

I run my fingers along the edges of the scissors, feel the sharp blade on my skin. A weapon, as cutting as a knife. That's how she must have experienced it when she cut deep into the cloth. A trickle of blood somewhere, invisible. Hurting, hurting.

And her, breathing hard, bent over the table, cutting, absorbed in her task, unaware of anything else. Her expert hands, with a mind of their own, working away.

She only stops when, sweating and exhausted, she has finished. She perhaps pushes her hair back from her forehead, wipes away the sweat with a handkerchief. She takes a deep breath now and smoothes her dress.

And then she goes out for a moment to buy some buttons, as if nothing had happened. As if she had done him a kindness and could announce calmly that evening: 'Ah, yes, that linen jacket I didn't have time to mend until now because my clients' work was more important, well, I've finally managed to sort it out.'

And he would perhaps say: 'Thank you.'

He might say that, because he wouldn't have seen and certainly couldn't have imagined: the first small tight stitches being ripped open by the scissors, and others meeting the same fate afterwards, torn out with one brusque, definitive gesture. The cotton wadding from the shoulder pads hanging out, the two or three rows of stitches in different colours around the armholes, the ragged edges fraying. The collar and the facings tossed aside, the sleeves taken out, each piece smaller than the next. Disconnected, all the threads broken. Especially the connecting thread, the master thread that united all the disparate pieces and transformed them into a whole.

I touch the inside of the jacket, touch the places where the seams once were. In one of the pockets something rustles, the cellophane wrapping from a packet of cigarettes. There's the smell of tobacco and the smell of your body on the light weave of the white linen, without its lining now. A summer jacket that bore the tailor's label. But the label has disappeared as well.

That night I lie awake for a long time, staring into the darkness, waiting for everyone else to fall asleep, then, finally, I go slowly downstairs, tiptoe along the corridor, enter the sewing room, pick up from the floor the scraps of silk and white lace left over from a blouse of Amélia's that is lying almost finished on top of the machine; I take pins, needles and threads from the round sandalwood box and put them in my pocket, along with the box of buttons, and go back upstairs to my room, as noiselessly as I came down.

Then I turn on the light and sit on the bed in order to make a doll out of the scraps and paint Amélia's face on it, copied patiently from a photograph I took from the album. Eyes and nose, mouth and eyebrows, and not forgetting her earrings, which I filched from her room during the day, and which I now sew on, one each side, where her ears would be. There can be no mistake; the doll looks just like her.

I'm not making a fetish to bring about her death, but one to send her away. On each hand and on each foot, on her ears and in the middle of her chest, I place a grain of salt. I scatter the pins around her to represent moonlight, I scatter white lace around her to represent the foaming waves.

The sea is going to carry her off, the same sea that brought her. And the lid of the button box is the boat in which she is seated.

I leave the sewing room and go over to the door that opens into the yard and I call on the *xipocués* – the spirits of the dead – to help me.

'Oh, winds that carry away the spirits, bring them to my house now, oh, winds that carry away the spirits, bring them to my house now, and make everything I wish for come true.'

The wind is blowing outside, the trees shiver with fear, shaking their leaves, the ground quakes beneath my feet, the breath of the *xipocués* strikes my face, my nightshirt clings to my body, I'm trembling with cold and burning up with heat as if I had a fever, but I can't turn back, I can't turn back now.

I go into the sewing room again. I place the box on which Amélia is sitting behind the door, underneath the wardrobe and, eyes closed, utter my silent plea:

'Go away and never come back. Never ever come back.'

2

This street was Avenida Duque de Connaught. A fine name that perfectly matched the stately mansions and the acacias, the casuarina trees and the sea. Behind it lay the Avenida Duquesa de Connaught, which was full of tall buildings, restaurants and boutiques. She enjoyed looking in the windows of those expensive shops, which started to appear more or less from Rua António Enes onwards.

That was where the city really began, near Rua António Enes and Rua Princesa Patrícia (or possibly even to the east of Rua Pero de Alenquer), extending as far as the cliff edge, as far as Bayly, Duquesa de Connaught and Duque de Connaught. And then it descended, almost vertically, to the sea below. In the distance, you could see the Clube Naval, the yachts and the other pleasure boats moored in the small harbour, and beside it the esplanade with tables and parasols. Coconut palms lined the coast road, along which cars passed in both directions, although more were heading towards the beach at Costa do Sol. The leaves of the palm trees swayed in the breeze.

She positioned herself more securely on the stone verandah, almost sitting on it, but keeping one foot on the ground, a position that at least gave her feet some respite from the high heels she was wearing, much too high for someone who had spent the whole of Sunday afternoon walking. But she hated flat shoes; the world was made to be traversed in high heels, which helped you to move more elegantly and your clothes to hang better, even if your feet suffered as a consequence. Fortunately, she thought, there were plenty of benches and she sat down on one, placing her marshmallow pink handbag beside her.

There were plenty of benches, especially in the streets facing the sea that had suddenly – or so it seemed to her – filled with sailing boats.

She had heard that at the Clube Naval, upon which she once again fixed her gaze, a luxury yacht had just arrived from Durban and was going to stay for a whole year before setting off on a round-the-world trip. It was a trimaran, a Victress, built in Capetown.

She had gleaned this from a conversation overheard between Dora Flávia and Graça Casaleiro, and when the latter had asked Dora how she knew, Dora had simply smiled and raised her eyebrows, as if to say that since she could only possibly have learned all this because she knew both the yacht and its owners, such a question was inappropriate and absurd.

The city proper began at Rua António Enes and Rua Princesa Patrícia, passed along Rua General Botha, through Parque José Cabral and the surrounding streets – Fernandes Tomás, Eduardo Costa, Couceiro da Costa, Belegarde da Silva, Massano de Amorim and a few others – and then continued down to the sea, as far as Ponta Vermelha, where Duquesa de Connaught, Fernandes Tomás and Belegarde da Silva all began.

That was what the avenues were like, long and broad, stretching for miles, but they could be misleading too. An address in Avenida 24 de Julho, for example, could as easily be a building bearing a sign announcing the Manzy Beauty Parlour or the Versailles Patisserie as some place at the other end of the avenue, where the city suddenly became the *caniço* – the shanty town. And there were other avenues, too, that wavered between those two extremes.

She, however, wasn't interested in that part of the city, with the possible exception of certain streets in the Baixa. That side existed solely in order to serve this one, perched high up and facing the sea. She would also include in the city the top of the hill and the view from the Hotel Cardoso or the Hotel Girassol. The rest, generally speaking, didn't count. At a certain point, as the avenues plunged into the tangled skein of the *caniço*, their geometry grew blurred, whereas this was never a danger with the 'real city', defended as it was by the sea.

Everything was defended here. The houses had massive gates and painted wrought-iron railings, and were hidden away behind trees, in the shade, camouflaged by ivy, bougainvillea and flowerbeds. They concealed the fact that they had two reception rooms, five bedrooms, a dining-room, three bathrooms, balconies, a study, a studio, lumber rooms, servants' quarters, a barbecue, two garages, and an enormous garden. Anyone passing by or sitting on a bench, as she was now, would see little more than the closed gate and, through the dark-green railings, a handyman watering the flowerbeds with a hosepipe with a metal spout.

Between the branches of the trees, you could make out only the upper portion of the façade, where there was a balcony and, beside it, an open window. If you looked really hard, you could, at most, see that the curtains framing the window were made of chintz and that on the balcony there was a rocking chair with striped yellow cushions on it.

And if, as was happening now, a boy opened the gate to let in a car, a metallic grey Alfa Romeo driven by a uniformed black chauffeur, you might catch a glimpse of the garden with the paving stones interspersed with grass that formed the driveway leading to the garage and a pergola at the far end. But the boy was already closing the gate again, and anyone watching would be left, as she was, sitting on a bench in the street, surrounded by the dry seed pods fallen from the acacia trees.

She looked at her watch and saw that it was gone five o'clock. She would have to walk quickly if she was to get home before they did, in time to change her clothes and sit down again at her sewing table, but she didn't feel like leaving just yet. It was a cool, pleasant September day. It would be light for at least another hour.

This was how she often spent her Sundays, strolling the streets or sitting by the sea. Her head was so full of things that she preferred to be alone. Only at the very last moment did she catch the bus and run home so that she would be there before them, sitting working as if she had never moved. It was a pointless lie, but she took pleasure in lying to them.

She looked at the palm trees down below. Perhaps everything in her life was a mistake, but there was no going back. It was as if, on the other side of the sea, where she came from, the world had ceased to exist. And in a way this was true: there was no going back.

The city had deceived her, which is why she hated it so much. No, it wasn't the city that had deceived her, it was life, yes, life had deceived her. The city was not so very different from how she had imagined it, indeed, it was possibly even prettier. She had dreamed of something just like this, the asphalt strip of the coast road, the gardens, the open parasols, the sailing boats, the beaches, the swimming pools. These things did exist, she could see them clearly, but they existed somewhere on the far horizon, beyond her reach.

She was on the margins, looking in, while life, like the sailing boats, passed her by. It was all so visible and real that she felt like crying, but crying only made matters worse, she thought, taking a paper handkerchief from her handbag. It was as if the world were laughing at her, as if the parasols, the houses, the boats, the trees and, above all, the people were laughing at her.

Half past five. She looked in her hand mirror, freshened her lipstick and tidied her hair. This was the latest she could leave it before going home.

The following Sunday, though, she would be back and would once more take up her position on a bench. The same one or a different one, it didn't matter, there were so many and so many places that looked out to sea.

There was the pergola covered in bougainvillea flowers, where she was now, there was the Miradouro and the Estrada do Caracol whose winding path she would sometimes follow down to the beach.

The sea was usually calm, with gentle waves, and not blue, as she had imagined, but grey-green, almost the colour of lead. You could walk along by the sea for miles; there was a broad promenade shaded by palm trees. When it was a cool afternoon and she had the breeze in her face, she felt as if she could walk all the way to Costa do Sol without even feeling tired, even though it was nearly eight miles or more.

On the beach, when the tide was out, the waves retreated and revealed a vast stretch of fine, white sand, but there wasn't much smell of the sea there. For that you had to go to Macaneta beach, where the sea was wilder and more intensely blue.

Actually, she never walked very far; there always came a moment when she felt tired and sat down on a bench, even though her desire to walk was still unsatisfied, a desire to walk all afternoon along a smooth beach, empty of people.

On Sundays, though, the beach was full, there were lots of people and lots of cars driving along the coast and she stayed where she was, high up among the bougainvillea flowers.

True, on Sundays, bus number 1 went as far as Costa do Sol, but she hated buses, just as she hated the people who travelled on them and went for picnics on the beach. She would rather look at the sea from afar and be alone.

At that hour, Dora Flávia would either be at the tennis club or the golf club. There was nothing on at the racetrack, and she wouldn't be going to the Jockey Club, she had said so to Conceição Santana or to Pureza Antelo over the phone. At least that's what she thought she'd heard her say. She heard a lot of things now that she went there to work every Wednesday.

She was always quick to warn her clients: 'I don't do fittings on Wednesdays. I have to go to Sommershild then.'

She said this for the sheer pleasure of linking the name of that elegant residential area with her own, for the pleasure of knowing that word would soon get around: 'Amélia's not here on Wednesdays.' Or: 'Amélia isn't here then, she'll be in Sommershild.'

She herself said it in an expressionless voice, as if it were a matter of indifference to her and of no significance: 'On Wednesdays I go to Sommershild.'

She had given no further explanation and had allowed a profound silence to settle over the subject. She never said that she went there to mend the children's clothes and, occasionally, to alter the maids' uniforms. She left space, in that silence and in the haughty expression on her face, for the assumption, or at least the suspicion, that she was making dresses for Dora, dresses that were, in fact, bought in Lisbon or other European cities, in South Africa or at the fashion shows held at the Hotel Polana. And if Dora was sent silks from Hong Kong or Macau, she would have some couturier make them up (Amélia hadn't yet heard any specific name mentioned, but wondered if it would be someone she had heard of, Maria Eunice perhaps or Madame Laurentina Borges).

Fortunately, right at the start, a chance incident had given support to the version of events that best suited her: Dora Flávia had asked her to sew up part of the hem of a dress that had come undone. It was late in the day and Amélia had suggested that she do the work at home. Dora had shrugged, saying that she really didn't mind, since she wouldn't be needing the dress immediately.

And so Amélia had taken the dress home with her and left it hanging up all week in her sewing room. And whenever she was doing a fitting, she would mention that she had to have the dress finished by next Wednesday. It belonged to the lady of the house. In Sommershild.

Usually, she didn't even have to draw attention to it. The dress spoke for itself and immediately attracted the gaze of her clients.

She had left it there, like a talisman that would free her from the world of cheap shops like A Feira or Lourenço Marques

Mercantil in Rua dos Irmãos Roby. As if the dress, on the clothes hanger, were an external sign of change.

She only sewed up the hem the following Tuesday night. This proved quite difficult because the muslin seemed to dissolve in her hands, but it was a pleasure, too, simply to touch that fabric – so soft and light that the word 'diaphanous' could have been invented for it.

Once it was ready, she tried it on. Their bodies were so alike, with the same measurements, and it looked even better on her; indeed, she thought herself considerably prettier than Dora. However, such dresses belonged to some women and not to others. Even if a woman cut them out and sewed them with her own hands, they still belonged to someone else. Lives could not be exchanged.

She knew that Dora would never pay her a fair price. No one would. Nor would she be able to explain. If she tried, in this case, to list the problems she had encountered, she would speak of the texture, as insubstantial as shifting sand, in which the pins and the needle kept slipping, and Dora would nod distractedly, assuming that Amélia was justifying asking a higher price for that extra work, and would say impatiently, yes, yes, without listening, because it made no difference to her if she paid a little less or a little more and, besides, the conversation bored her. Amélia would never be able to explain that the problem hadn't been the work itself, but the tightness in her throat, as if an iron hand were gripping it, leaving her unable to breathe.

She could make a dress exactly like this, she thought, twirling round in front of the mirror. She would be perfectly capable of making one, identical down to the last stitch; and yet, however close, however feasible such a project seemed, it was, at the same time, quite impossible. Unreal. Even if such fabric were available in the shops there and even if she could afford it (both these things were equally unlikely), she would never have a chance to wear it, because she didn't have access to the kind of places where such clothes were worn.

Still standing in front of the mirror, she slowly took the dress off. How could she ever have enjoyed those visits to Sommershild, enjoyed what she had called, in her initial euphoria, 'the Sommershild era'? How could she have been so mad as to have believed that her life would change, simply because she had started going regularly to a particular place?

Then again, it had been such a new and surprising experience to cross the city and enter the other side, as if, by some miracle, the ancient bus were carrying her, jolting and bumping, towards what had always been her secret goal. Her heart had beat faster when the gates opened for the first time and she went up the steps and in through the front door, when she walked in her high heels over the black-and-white marble floor of the hall.

The house had opened up to her like a world, which, from that moment on, she would know from the inside: the dining room, the kitchen and the pantry, the large reception room upstairs that gave onto the long balcony, the children's rooms, the guest room, the bedroom occupied by Dora Flávia and her engineer husband, with its en suite bathroom all in marble and with lamps over the mirrors, the games room, the engineer's study, the barbecue in the garden, the ping-pong table in the porch beside the garage and the rooms set aside for the staff.

The house opened up to her as it opened to the girls who did the ironing, to errand boys and to cleaners. It seemed so close that you only had to reach out your hand to touch it, and yet it remained, at the same time, utterly inaccessible, as if protected by a glass screen.

Life was not to be trusted, it set traps into which she carelessly fell.

No, life was not to be trusted. Now and then you did something just for the fun of it, gave in to an urge to do something crazy, like reading your future in the cards, in shells, bones or cigarette ash, or writing letters to complete strangers. There were times when you just couldn't stand it any longer and succumbed to foolish whims, infatuations, impulses. And that was fine, it was your business and nobody else's.

But life decided to take you seriously and, having caught you making that first step, forced you to keep on walking. It wasn't right, but life was like that. Because of one small step, taken just for the hell of it, you could find yourself on the other side of the world, almost without knowing how. And then there was no turning back.

She had embarked in Lisbon at around eleven o'clock one winter morning. The first and only time she saw the Jerónimos monastery and the Torre de Belém was from that ship, at a considerable distance, and they were nothing like the photos she had seen, they seemed so small and unreal, especially the Torre de Belém, which looked as if it were made out of sugar, just like the little model she had once seen on top of a cake.

Despite the fine rain that was falling, she stayed up on deck to catch a glimpse of the city, which she had always longed to see and never had, but Lisbon soon vanished, swallowed by the mist, and all that was left was the sea, the grey sky and the cries of the seagulls that accompanied the ship and occasionally dived down into the water.

The sea grew rough as soon as they crossed the harbour bar; she immediately felt unwell and was sick right there on the deck. She had great difficulty getting down to her cabin, stumbling and being thrown against the walls of corridors and stairways and dropping her handbag – the clink of coins falling, a hand mirror breaking, the lipstick, which, at the time, she didn't even think to look for and never found again. When she reached the café, broken crockery and fallen chairs were slithering across the floor and crashing into the walls. She instinctively grabbed hold of one of the tables, which didn't fall over, presumably because it was fixed to the floor.

She spent the whole sleepless night retching. Far worse than her fear was the awful feeling of nausea, with the bile constantly rising up into her mouth, and the sense that someone was committing an act of violence on her from which she could not escape.

If only the rocking motion would stop and the ship would stay still, however briefly, because then she could take a deep breath and put stomach and body in their proper place. She might be able to withstand the motion better afterwards if she had a moment, a single moment, of relief, like on a car journey when you can open the window and feel the air on your face or, if that doesn't work, stop by the roadside and feel solid ground beneath your feet. But on board ship there was nowhere to escape to, there was only the sea and the sky, which appeared alternately in the porthole, now that day was breaking.

She closed her eyes and lay very still, as if she were dead. If she could manage to feign death, she thought, the feelings of nausea might abate.

In the bunk beneath hers, an old nun was praying; Amélia could hear her mumbled Hail Marys, intercut by faint whistling sounds when, for a moment, she forgot to pray and fell asleep. A younger nun kept getting up from the bunk opposite to give the older one some water or orange juice to drink and to see if she was feverish. A sour smell filled the air, the heat was suffocating, even though it was winter, some juice had been spilled on the floor and a bottle of water lay broken; the nun moaned softly; the screams of children came through the wall; suitcases clattered to the floor in the neighbouring cabin; and from outside came the sound of loud voices and slamming doors.

She turned over in bed, sweaty and grubby and filled by an intense desire to cry. She swore to herself that she would never ever get on a boat again or drink orange juice, not as long as she lived.

The journey was getting off to a bad start, she thought. The fact that the first step taken towards that new land had already brought her only suffering was surely a bad omen.

Perhaps it was just chance that a life like Dora Flávia's was not awaiting her on her arrival at the quay. Possibly, but how could she have known that beforehand?

The idea had occurred to her when she passed the engineer on the stairs and he greeted her with a faint smile and a nod, the idea that it could have been him waiting for the steamship she was travelling on. He could have been the one who had placed that advertisement in the newspaper.

It would have taken just one tiny thing for her life to have been entirely different – answering a different advertisement, happening upon a different page in the newspaper.

Perhaps that's why she was so fascinated by those two or three line ads on which people gambled their lives. She sometimes cut them out and put them in her needle drawer and only long afterwards did she throw them away. She kept them not because she intended replying, but because they were so intriguing: 'Young woman, twenty-five, seeks gentleman for spiritual comfort.'

The personal ads and the horoscopes were always the sections she turned to first. On the day she had started going to Sommershild, her horoscope had said: 'The big event is going to be the appearance of the Dragon's Tail in your sign on the 26th. An unexpected, but long-hoped-for change this week will mark the beginning of a new stage in your life.'

He had written the advertisement, it was true. He had given the matter great thought because such things were difficult to do well and he had ended up writing: 'Gentleman, single, hard-working and honest, 30 years old, resident in Mozambique, seeks decent young woman aged 25 max., with view to marriage. Please send photograph, which will be returned if unsuitable. Only serious applicants need apply. Write to L.C. P.O. Box No. . . . Lourenço Marques, Mozambique.'

However, when he re-read this, he was filled with anxiety. It was just like any other ad. How could the woman he was hoping to meet feel that those words went straight to her heart, how would it make her open the newspaper and feel her blood beating hard, as happens when we come face to face with fate? There were many paths to love, he believed, but the parties concerned needed a good heart and God's blessing.

On an impulse he added: 'If you trust in God that you will meet your ideal partner and build a happy home, then write to me. I'm waiting for you.' And he had put his name: Laureano Capítulo.

It had been complete chance. Neither she nor Conceição nor Celeste knew exactly where Mozambique was. They looked on the map and when she alighted on the name 'Porto Amélia', they all burst out laughing because it seemed so perfect. Porto Amélia. She would get off the boat in a place that bore her name, and she would look for the man waiting for her on the quay in the city that lay at her feet.

It was fate knocking at the door, they said, laughing, and it didn't matter if the husband-to-be would, in fact, be waiting for her at another port, in the country's capital city.

But they were just playing with the idea; after all, she had come across the advertisement in the newspaper entirely by accident. No one in her godmother's house read newspapers. The advertisement had turned up by chance, on a page that had been used to wrap up a pair of shoes belonging to Uncle Alfredo, who had arrived a few days before on a visit.

She carried the shoes into the kitchen and spread the newspaper out on the table. That was when she read it. She didn't know that the one small step she took between kitchen and living room, where she read the advertisement out loud to Conceição and Celeste, would be the beginning of a great journey.

At the time, the only thing she knew was that she wanted to annoy Joaquim. It was purely because of him that she wrote this letter three weeks later:

Dear Senhor Capítulo,
I am writing to say that I have read your advertisement. I am nineteen and have lived with my godmother since I was six. I enclose my photograph as requested.
Amélia dos Santos Marcelino.

It had all been Joaquim Albano's fault, because of a stupid quarrel. She had wanted to make him jealous, really jealous, with a genuine suitor, who would have her cross the oceans to meet him unless Joaquim was man enough to grab her first.

Joaquim would sometimes behave like a complete fool and get jealous for no reason, and at times she felt like throttling him.

'Zé Furna can't keep his eyes off you and well you know it, so don't go playing the innocent, because I've got eyes in my head too.' And one way or another, he made her life a misery all through Carnival. She had told him that she never wanted to speak to him again, because if he was going to spend his life inventing men to be jealous of, he could clear off and forget all about her.

And so Carnival passed, as did Lent. On Easter Sunday, she tried to patch things up, but Joaquim was still sulking. No one could persuade him that she hadn't been making eyes at Zé Furna, despite Zé Furna swearing blind that she hadn't and her screaming at him that he, Joaquim Albano, was the man she loved, but that she would stop loving him altogether if he carried on like this.

But Joaquim refused to back down and apologise for being so stupid and inventing problems that didn't exist, and instead he started pursuing Adelina or pretending that he was, and all to make Amélia jealous.

And so since he was pretending to be seriously courting Adelina, Amélia decided to pretend that she was seriously thinking of leaving for Africa.

That was when she had the photograph taken, and because she rarely sat for photos and because the idea amused her, she curled her hair with paper curlers for several days prior to the sitting, having first applied camomile tea to bring out the colour, which went from light brown to almost blonde, especially at the front, framing her face. And so that news of this would spread and reach Joaquim's ears, she consulted Elisa on which dress suited her best, but ended up wearing one of Celeste's blouses, with a little lace edging round the neck.

In the end, her new blonde look went unnoticed, because the photo was in black and white, and the waves in her hair were barely noticeable either. But there were the lace edging and her smiling face, and she was, on the whole, satisfied with the result.

Anyway, she decided, as she sealed the envelope, she wasn't going to spend any more money on the affair. All she needed was to make sure that Joaquim found out if she proved to be the chosen one.

And so that the news would spread and reach Joaquim's ears, she used to read out the letters she received to her girlfriends:

The city was very beautiful, by the sea, with a port much larger than Lisbon's and a bay many miles long and wide; on the far side lay Catembe, which you reached in a boat called a ferry; you could see the island of Xefina most of the time from many points in the city and Inhaca Island too, but only on a clear day. And there were other places to visit too, which he was sure she would enjoy. And as for the rest, she would also like – had she ever seen a monkey? A zebra? A crocodile? A huge rubber tree? A papaya tree?

The letters duly became the subject of gossip, and she had the feeling that people in the village were taking more interest in her, that she was somehow more real to them because she was corresponding with someone. This pleased her, for she had long felt a kind of secret rage, a desire to avenge herself on the world. She'd had to swallow her godmother's charity since she was six. Charity was all very well, of course, but she was really little more than a servant.

Her godmother kept saying that she loved Amélia like a daughter, but she treated her real daughter, Palmira, quite differently.

Ah, and there was more to that business of being like a daughter than met the eye. Maybe she had been like a daughter to her godfather Honorato, who, shortly before he died, had given her the pocket watch he kept by his bedside, a gold watch that had been his one luxury. It wasn't worth much, he said, but it was something to remember him by.

She was about eleven when he died and she had cried a lot, although mainly in secret because, it seemed, neither her godmother nor Palmira liked to see her cry, as if the right to grieve and mourn were theirs alone. They wouldn't even let her wear black, she was too young, they said, and insisted on her wearing a white blouse with her skirt.

She still had the watch at the back of her drawer. It had been such a strange feeling. She had always believed that he loved her, but had put this down to kindness on his part or to old age and was genuinely surprised by that gesture. He was very ill and in bed, and he beckoned her over to him, put the gold watch in her hand, closing her fingers over it and patting them gently. 'It's not worth very much,' he managed to say, 'but it's something to remember me by.' He tried to smile, but was too overcome by emotion to say anything more.

Those were his last words because he must then have taken a turn for the worse, although no one noticed, they were all standing round the bed in silence, numb with shock. Only afterwards did they realise how ill he was and called for the doctor and began their weeping and wailing.

A few days after his death, no one said anything more about it.

Later on, though, her godmother would say very coolly: 'Fancy giving the watch to Amélia. He obviously didn't know what he was doing by then because he always told me it was to go to Palmira.' Then she would cross herself and add: 'But what's given is given, and far be it from me to change things because, who knows, he might well have been in his right mind at the time and really meant to give it to her. Well, he was a very kind-hearted man, and we've always spoiled Amélia dreadfully.'

You can go to Bilene, a beach with pale sand dunes and clear, clear water. Or to Namaacha, where you can sit in the cool under the trees, even in summer, and where there's a waterfall that cascades down onto huge rocks and which you can reach on foot, by crossing a bridge.

The watch made her wonder sometimes if she really was her godfather's daughter. The village gossips used to talk about it under their breath, but always loud enough for her to hear, saying that she had been born on the wrong side of the blanket and was the daughter of that unfortunate creature who had all those fatherless children, although she's long gone now, may God forgive her. So maybe she *was* his daughter, just like Palmira.

Perhaps in order to hide this fact, her godmother was eager to tell anyone who would listen how faithful her husband had always been and how, in forty years of marriage, he had never given her a moment's grief. This was quite a different story from the one told by the gossips, especially Rosa, Marta and Alice when they went to do their washing at the village wash-house. According to them, Honorato was no saint and had even been with Joana Coxa from Olival de Cima.

After her godfather died, everything changed very much for the worse. Her godmother got annoyed with her over the slightest thing and seemed to be angry all the time.

The watch, therefore, brought her nothing but misfortune. It became for her the sign of an injustice, a sign that she had a right to other things, that life had defrauded her. She was filled with rage at her godmother, at Palmira and even more so at her godfather Honorato.

She often thought that she should throw the wretched thing away, and the only reason she hadn't done so was because that wouldn't stop her remembering.

The letters came and went, and she began to grow dizzy, as if she were going round and round on a fairground carousel. And there were certain words that seemed to be whirling around behind her:

'He seems such a nice lad and none of us here is likely to strike it rich.' 'Don't throw away a piece of good luck when it comes your way.'

You can go on trips to Bela Vista, Ponta Mahone, Ponta do Ouro and other places. The Komati river has lots of small islands as well as larger ones inhabited by fishermen, and you get there by raft, on the way to Macaneta beach, and once there – as close as going from wherever you're sitting now to the door of your house or garden – all you can see is sand and river.

And before you knew it, the flirtation between Joaquim and Adelina appeared to be getting serious, and perhaps it really was.

She despaired then and sent him a note: 'Joaquim, the letters don't mean anything, it was just a way of having my revenge on you. If you still love me, come to my window tonight.'

She waited all night for him to throw a stone up at the window, as he used to. She would have opened it and let him in, and he would have slept with her, as he had done before. And they would have made their peace with each other. As they had also done before.

But no stone struck her window.

Laureano still had the letter he had received from the godmother. It was there, along with Amélia's letters, on the top shelf in the wardrobe, in the large sandalwood box:

Dear Senhor Capítulo,
I hope this finds you in perfict health as it finds me thank God –

Even though she had waited all night, tormenting herself and thinking of a thousand reasons why he didn't come: perhaps he hadn't got her note, perhaps her godmother was spreading rumours about her, perhaps she had her suspicions about the previous nights they'd spent together and had barred the way or taken to patrolling the house, wielding her umbrella.

Im riting to you, sir, not becos you asked for informashun about Amélia who replyed to what you put in the newzpaper, but I wud not have felt at eez with my conshuns if I had alowed her to make the jurney without giving you that informashun becos Im shure you want to know, even tho you havnt asked, we women know what men are like, they never trust us women and dout our onesty becos looking for a wife is a serius bizness and marrying at a distens is different from marrying somone from here in the village, well I was married to my Honorato God rest him for fourty years and always very happy too but I just wanted to say that Amélia is a serius God-feering girl like girls used to be from a good famly too very honest and with many good qualites and never been courted by no one and whoever takes her to the alter will find in her a good wife and wont regret it for a moment becos when I was taken bad she always treeted me like I was her mother and I never lacked for nothing wich is why I love her like a dauter and not just becos shes my goddauter becos yung peepul nowadays are not like they use to be but you can rest esy on that frunt becos shes a good respecful girl and a good housekeeper too and very hard-workin and cleen and the priest who batized her can give you more informashun if you need it but Im not lyin when I say that I wud put my hand in the fier for her goodby Senhor Capitulo may God keep you in his grace, yours

Maria do Livramento de Nossa Senhora Coelho

Her godmother was pushing her, everyone was pushing her, while she wept and looked for Joaquim, but Joaquim avoided her and, on the one occasion when they did meet, he told her bluntly that he didn't love her because he didn't trust her, and this only made her cry all the more and feel as if she were somehow cursed or not in her right mind.

They were pushing her and she was going. She would have preferred them to have shoved her down a well; at least, that way, it would all be over.

Everything happened very quickly and smoothly, as if the die were cast and things could not now be any different.

He had been touched by her fate: orphaned at six years old and sent to live with her godmother, where she had learned to sew and do the housework. Perhaps she did her sewing while sitting at the window, looking out on the village square, but not liking any of the boys who passed. Not knowing that he was waiting for her, far away in Africa. That was what life and destiny were like.

He sent her some money to sort out the paperwork, buy a gold chain and a ring and a few clothes if she wanted, 'but mainly summer clothes, because, like I said, it's pretty hot here'.

Because of Joaquim she had still corresponded, years later, with Celeste, who had gone to live in Oporto, but still kept in touch with village life. She worded the letters very carefully and cautiously. How's this person and that person, she always asked at the end, but never mentioned Joaquim, as if he simply didn't exist.

And only in her sixth letter, in a PS, as if it were the last thing on her mind, did she ask: 'What's happened to Graciana? And João Rolo? And Palmira?' then, right at the bottom of the page, in tiny letters: 'And what about Joaquim?'

Finally, she thought, as she sealed the envelope, she had finally asked the question that justified those six letters. She had to know whether or not he had married Adelina. And it was with great excitement that she read the reply that arrived two months and eighteen days later: 'Graciana married Augusto and lives in Cimo do Olival, Zé Rolo and Inácia are in Gaia, Palmira is still single, and Joaquim married Adelina, they've got a little girl, and now that his father-in-law is dead, he's in charge of the grocer's shop.'

She threw away the letter and cried all afternoon. At Christmas, though, she wrote a long letter back to Celeste ('we have three servants and a cook') and enclosed a postcard showing the Hotel Polana reflected in the swimming pool ('this is where we spent our honeymoon and my husband takes me to a dinner-dance here every Saturday').

She also included a photograph of the casuarina trees along the coast road where you could see two monkeys scrambling along a branch, because people seemed to be impressed by monkeys and they were always a favourite with village folk.

After that, she never wrote again.

Sometimes, though, it was like reaching the bottom of a well and rising up again to the surface. 'Nonsense,' she would think. 'What was so wonderful about life in the village? And I wasn't *so* very much in love with Joaquim. He was far too jealous and not much of a man, he had no guts. Maybe it wasn't my godmother's fault after all. That's how things turned out and there's nothing more to be said. Besides, it's hardly the high life, working in a grocer's shop, nor is digging the fields, which is what he'd be doing if we'd stayed together. Anyway, it's all water under the bridge.'

The following day, the sea grew calmer and the wind dropped. They had already passed Cabo Branco and Dakar and were heading for São Tomé.

The sky took on a pale, milky tone with the occasional patch of blue. On the first-class deck, which she could see in the distance, people were sitting in deckchairs, reading. Others wore sunglasses or were smoking or scanning the horizon through binoculars. She got to know the couple in the cabin next to hers. They had been to Portugal on holiday and had a little girl called Orlanda. According to them, some ships even had a swimming pool in first class, although theirs did not.

They reached São Tomé when it was gone midnight, and so all they could see was a string of lights. The engines stopped, the night was calm and silent, as if the ship were a hotel. In the morning she saw the green island and the mountains, and heard, with some displeasure, that they were going to spend the whole day there. Almost all the passengers disembarked in order to take the boat to Ana Chaves Bay. Then, said the couple, as they set off with Orlanda, they would hire a taxi and go for a drive around the island. Would Amélia like to come too? To visit the village of Água Izé? No, she wouldn't. She didn't have enough money to go spending it on taxis. Well, she didn't actually say that, but it was what she felt. The day turned out to be long, hot and tedious.

That evening, they set sail again. Was there going to be another long stopover like that, she asked a sailor, and immediately regretted the question because it made her feel so ignorant. She should have found that out before getting on the wretched boat, which might be taking the slowest of all possible routes.

He answered with what she thought was a mocking smile. Of course there would be more stops. In Luanda, Lobito and Capetown. She would be able to get off the boat there as well.

She smiled too – to hide her anger. At this rate, they would never arrive.

'Why the hurry?' he asked. On board ship, every day was a party. And he told her about a ball that had been held in first class, and how some passengers had been invited to drink champagne in the captain's cabin. They had even sung *fados*, which you could hear from out in the corridor.

And what else, what else, she wanted to know, greedy for news.

He laughed. Well, before that there was supper served with punch, and the guests danced tangos and waltzes in the ballroom. The women wore beautiful long dresses and the men sweated in their dinner jackets, because it was very hot, despite the air-conditioning.

The pain of being excluded. There were, it seemed, forbidden places, doors that only opened to the few. That was how it was, and the far-off fiancé who had summoned her to Africa wouldn't be opening any of those doors for her.

And what else, what else, she asked, as if wanting to gauge the full extent of her misfortune.

He laughed again, enjoying being in the privileged position of witness, having walked around the room with a tray, serving drinks.

At midnight, they had let off streamers and blown whistles, as if it were New Year's Eve, and, as they danced, a hat was passed round from head to head. The person who ended up with the hat when the music stopped had to find a new partner.

And the following day, he said, they would be crossing the Equator and anyone doing so for the first time would be ritually sprinkled with water. They called it a baptism.

After the Equator, we'll be heading for the Tropic of Capricorn, the seas of Capricorn, she had thought. Ships sailed across the sea as if through the astrological houses — would that signify a change, she wondered.

'And how's the seasickness?' he said, laughing. 'You'll be sick again when we round the Cape of Good Hope. Mind you, the prow to stern motion isn't the worst. The worst is port to starboard, like it was when we left Lisbon.'

She preferred Moçâmedes, where they did not disembark, to Luanda, where passengers could leave the ship and go into the city, which was a long way from the quay; she preferred Moçâmedes, of which you could see only an arid, desolate strip of land, to the clear blue bay of Lobito. At least no one disembarked in Moçâmedes. At most, someone leant over the side and did a little fishing to pass the time.

She also stayed on the ship in Capetown (as she'd heard other people call it, rather than Cidade do Cabo). She saw the high mountains, their tops veiled in cloud, and, at night, the bright broad swathe of lights. 'It looks like New York,' said someone who had been there. 'It's all very splendid and modern, and the buildings are as tall as skyscrapers.'

And then the ship began rolling again, and again she was sick. It wasn't quite so bad as before, but she still couldn't sleep. In the morning she saw the Indian Ocean — vast and syrupy and flecked with foam. Would this be her sea from now on? She found it uglier than the Atlantic, but calmer. There she was wrong again. It started to rain hard and the sea grew rough and wild, with large waves crashing into the boat, clashing with each other and exploding in great bursts of foam.

Outside Durban, the wind died down again. She heard someone say that the first-class passengers would be holding one last ball because tomorrow the ship was due to arrive in Lourenço Marques. They had been at sea for almost twenty days.

111

Now that she was almost there, she felt afraid. Part of her wished that the ship would sail on and on and never arrive.

He had fixed up the house. He tackled one job every day when he got back from work. With a cigarette in the corner of his mouth and sometimes a pencil behind his ear. Whistling to himself. He loved working with his hands, it relaxed him, he enjoyed seeing how applying new materials could completely change the look of things.

He put green linoleum down on the bathroom floor, replaced the piece of wire around the bathtub with a chrome shower rail on which he hung a plastic curtain decorated with blue and red balls.

The kitchen was improved by the addition of a round formica-topped table and two chairs, as well as some fresh paint on the wall, which needed a second coat on the chimney breast. He chose white to brighten up the room because the kitchen, having only one small window, was rather dark, its main source of light being the door that opened out into the yard. For the bedroom, though, he chose beige and for the living room a light green that went well with the sofa cushions.

Once the living room was ready, he felt that the walls looked rather bare and thought it would be a good idea to put up some pictures. He bought some from a little black boy of about ten, who was selling them in the street: a woman with her back to the viewer, carrying a bucket of water on her head and holding a child by the hand. They were walking along a narrow path that rose and disappeared into the jungle beyond. The other painting showed some leaves, branches, tall scrub and the head of a lion peering out. You couldn't see the rest of its body, which was hidden by the scrub. He hung them side by side, carefully measuring the distance between floor and nail.

Also for the living room, he bought a collection of locally made statuettes, which he placed the shelves of the book-case, and a lampstand to put next to the aviator's chair. This required him to fit a new wall socket, with the wires carefully disguised, pulling them through from the box up by the ceiling, then fitting them round the doorframe and along the skirting board.

He picked up other things here and there, as and when, sometimes paying for them in instalments, so as not to overstretch his budget, for example, the bright red damask bedspread for the double bed, two rugs, both the same, one on either side of the bed, and another different one for the hall.

The city didn't have many furniture shops, and so there was very little choice, but nevertheless he also bought, at the last moment, an umbrella stand and a little table that he happened to find, and which he liked and bought simply because it was made of an unusual wood – chamfuti or pod mahogany – and even though he couldn't find an immediate use for it. In a house destined to become a family home there was bound to be some use for a table like that.

It wasn't at the Cape of Good Hope but at Cape Agulhas that the Atlantic ended and the Indian Ocean began, a sailor told her when she went up on deck at the close of day.

He himself had been up on the cliffs and seen some of the unbelievable places that all the tourist groups visited – Da Gama Park, False Bay and then, in the distance, Cape Agulhas, the exact point where the waters divide, with the huge waves of the unpredictable, stormy Atlantic on one side and the calm, gentle Indian Ocean on the other.

Oh, there was a lot to see in South Africa, cities that disappeared in winter beneath huge snowfalls, ghostly mining settlements, not to mention Capetown itself, surrounded by mountains and greenery, and Table Mountain with its table-cloth of clouds. If she had the opportunity, she must be sure to visit – how long was she staying?

At first, she didn't know what to say because she found the question so frightening.

'I'm not sure,' she said at last, her heart pounding, feeling as if she would never say a true word about herself again. 'I've come to visit relatives, for a holiday.'

He smiled. 'So the length of visit depends on whether or not you like it here?'

She smiled back and nodded.

He had pale eyes, she noticed, and was tall and thin. He could pass for a foreigner. And that uniform suited him, set off his tanned skin.

He had placed the advertisement in the newspaper as if he were putting a message in a bottle and throwing it into the sea. He felt sad afterwards, but didn't know why.

In the days that followed, he had walked the streets after work to avoid thinking about it. Once the step had been taken, there was no going back.

He remembered a story someone had told him. A woman received in the post a response to a letter she had placed in a bottle and thrown into the sea twelve years before, when she was still a child. With the answer came her original message, surprisingly well preserved, despite, as she found out later, its incredible journey. The bottle containing the letter had floated from the Dutch coast to the North Sea, past Norway, then drifted about in the Arctic, floated down to Canada and been propelled by the Labrador Current towards France. Had he heard that somewhere or dreamed it?

His dreams that night were very confused. In the morning, all he could remember was the sea bursting in, shattering the window and filling the house with a sense of terrible anxiety.

She never did go to Capetown, she thought, as she sat beneath the pergola and its purple bougainvilleas. She never did see, from close to, the tablecloth of clouds draped over Table Mountain.

Yet she had met, or could say she had met, people for whom Europe seemed very close and South Africa a mere suburb just two steps away, people who 'used' South Africa in the same way that South Africans 'used' Mozambique, by adding Gorongosa, Santa Catarina and other places to their list of tourist destinations.

People who came and went and never felt trapped, who never ran the risk of feeling seasick on ships, instead – as easily as putting on a change of clothes – their plane would touch down gently at Mavalane airport and they would walk elegantly down some metal steps. Then they would get into a car, carrying only a small crocodile- or antelope-skin bag, possibly monogrammed, or, if the person in question was a woman, holding a vanity case in a modern design, its rounded corners edged in metal.

People who took their seat in the back of the car and didn't move, waiting for the chauffeur to run round, cap in hand, to close the door for them. People who drove through red lights and sped down the avenues, who changed their car as often as they changed their shoes and who enjoyed life everywhere, who knew what they should and shouldn't wear, who they should mix with, who they should despise, because, as she was discovering, the games played by that exclusive world were many and complex. It was a world that very few people entered and in which few stayed for very long. She was sure that a mere nothing – a laugh, a gesture, a nod of the head – was enough for them to tell at once, among themselves, who was worth knowing: those who didn't believe in the local celebrities in the fields of surgery, midwifery and cosmetic dentistry made fun of people who embarked on the rather down-market ship, the *Lúrio*, on cheap excursions to South African doctors organised by Luzáfrica, complete with interpreter and guide; they scorned those who stayed in the Johannesburg hotels where Portuguese was spoken, like the Grande or the Sherborne Hotel at 63 Claim Street. And from the

115

way they said the names of the streets – Eloff, Von Brandis, Pritchard – you would think they were their personal property, in daily usage; and the Lourenço Marques branch of John Orr was, for them, as nothing compared with the John Orr 'there', not to speak of the sheer abundance of goods to be bought at the OK Bazaar.

And when, by chance, instead of hopping on the first plane, they travelled by train to South Africa, their name would appear in the newspaper, under the heading 'Train Travel', as if the timetable were regulated by the frequency with which they packed their bags, and as if their comings and goings were the sole reason for the trains to run.

For Dora Flávia and her friends, their participation in charity tombolas and dog shows, in the sweepstake held at the Jockey Club, in international events held at the racetrack, was a concession they made to petty local life. They scorned the beaches in Mozambique and, every summer, left with their husbands and children in search of South African waters, which were so much cooler, breezier and foamier.

At home, they had air-conditioning units, which, as they put it, created a European climate in Africa. They thus controlled the climate and could almost change geography. Everything, even the climate (she saw now), was simply a matter of having enough money.

But even South Africa had become too monotonous and ordinary for them.

They had been to Capetown so often, Dora complained down the phone to Paulina Gameiro. She was encouraging Manuel Carlos and Leonor Garrido to go on a cruise to Japan. No, they were going to put their names down with the Albatroz travel agency. Well, they had to know who was going first. Or else organise a group. Marta Lobo? No, she hadn't said anything to her about it. Perhaps Sara and António Crespo?

It seemed to Amélia that Dora's friends had strange names and a special ability to scatter them around, as if they were floral arrangements or cherries in a basket from which, if you pulled out one, the others would follow. When you heard the name 'Sara Crespo' for example, you immediately thought 'Vidigal Nino' because that was her full name, and you felt impelled to say the whole thing, as if otherwise you were uttering a meaningless sentence: Sara Crespo Vidigal Nino. Or so at least it seemed to Amélia.

The names amused her. A name alone was enough to conjure up an image of the whole person, and she was usually right. Pureza Antelo was the oldest member of the group and she did look very pure and stiff, although she did not, as Amélia had imagined, wear her hair pinned up at the back in a kind of bun the shape of a banana. Her eyes were her most striking feature, for she drew a thin black line above her eyelashes and applied blue or green shadow to her lids depending on what colour she was wearing.

Telma Dias Marques was, as she had thought, rather younger and laughed a lot; she had a small gap between her front teeth and wore dark red lip gloss. She sometimes appeared slightly unsure of herself, as if she wasn't convinced that she had been entirely accepted.

For there was a fierce side to that world as well, which she found equally fascinating, like the claws of some wild animal. Many people were never admitted to certain circles or were admitted only to be excluded again later; there were those who waited day after day for an invitation that never came, while some proffered an invitation that the invitees elegantly declined or else accepted as a mere formality, but never reciprocated.

It looked so simple to an outsider, as if there were nothing more to that life than sitting on the verandah in chairs upholstered with floral cushions and playing canasta, bridge or mah-jong, eating scones and jam and drinking tea poured from silver teapots by black hands wearing white gloves.

It all looked so simple, but it wasn't. She heard, for example, that the dresses worn at the parties held at the Clube Naval and especially at the Grémio had been deemed too flashy or too vulgar (there were those who had looked splendid and others who were a complete disaster, those who knew which colours suited them and those who hadn't the faintest idea what jewels to wear when and which jewels suited their personality; there were those who knew how to draw up a menu when they received guests at home, something they all took turns at doing, well, it was a way of passing the time: vichyssoise (for example) and vol au vent was acceptable, but only someone with no taste and no imagination would serve their visitors prawn or lobster curry.

And beneath this idle, brilliant world lay another hidden one made up of hatred, rivalry, envy and jealousy; there were the love affairs, nights spent at gaming tables or in each other's houses, there was the drinking, the scandals, the fortunes lost at poker.

Oh, she knew, she knew all about it, and how those stories excited her, those tales heard through half-open doors, the scraps of phone conversations when she was measuring the children up for their clothes, and Graça Casaleiro or Telma or Paulina phoned and Dora interrupted the fitting of a dress for Maria, some shorts for Diogo or a smock for Martim and promised to phone right back, but then, unable to contain herself, spoke just one or two sentences, then half of another, and Amélia could glean quite a lot from the little that was said and even more from what was not, as if she could read clearly between the lines.

Dora felt free to say such things in front of her, just as she did in front of the cooks, the servants and the cleaners, because none of them existed: they were things, shadows, objects that passed through the house and would be thrown out tomorrow, as if they had never been there.

She was treated like a maid (nothing had changed, absolutely nothing, since she had lived in her godmother's house), she was treated like the black servants, and one day when Dora gave her some material for a blouse – an ugly fabric that, for some absurd reason, had ended up in her hands but that she didn't want to keep, which is why she was giving it to Amélia, as a more discreet way of throwing it in the rubbish – Amélia felt herself blush, as if she were barefoot in the jungle and her white bosswoman had just given it to her as a tip.

He sat down in the aviator's chair and looked around. The room had definitely changed for the better, it looked quite different. He just had to get rid of the rubbish he had allowed to accumulate in the meantime – tins of paint, bits of wire, tools scattered on the floor.

He would do that later. He closed his eyes and leaned back. It was a hot Sunday afternoon. Hot and sultry. He was sweating, his mouth was dry, and he was filled by a great weariness.

'What I need is a nice cool beer,' he thought. But it seemed too much of an effort to stand up, go to the kitchen, open the fridge and get the bottle-opener out of the drawer. He saw himself performing these gestures, but lacked the energy to carry them out.

He folded his arms, settled himself more comfortably in the chair, and prepared himself to sleep.

She liked names. They could reveal a lot about people, like photographs. For example, she liked the name Alegna d'Ortsac.

Alegna d'Ortsac gave beauty advice in a newspaper (Amélia always read her column immediately after she had read her horoscope) and was the owner of a salon of the same name, where you could enjoy a Turkish bath or have any unwanted body hair painlessly removed by electrolysis.

Amélia had always wanted to go to a beauty salon and had even saved up money to do so – just once, she told herself, she could afford to go just once. Even if she never went back there again. In the end, though, she had always felt too intimidated.

She looked at the names on the signs as she passed (Salão Rosa, Salão Lídia, Salão Tulipa) or that she came across by chance in some advertisement or leaflet – Carlos, *Haute Coiffure*, the hairdresser ladies go to for quality and perfection. (You had to make an appointment and it was in Avenida Massano de Amorim.) Or Salão Veneza, Salão Arcádia, in the atrium of the Nauticus building. There was also the Instituto de Beleza Adelina, but she would never go there, the name 'Adelina' was a fateful name as far as she was concerned.

If she were ever to visit a salon, she would choose the one owned by Alegna d'Ortsac. She wondered what Alegna would be like, if she could find inspiration in her or copy her like a fashion plate. Alegna, she decided, would be tall and slender and would wear a wine-red dress. She would speak slowly with a marked foreign accent. Alegna could be what? Italian, she thought. Or perhaps she was a Montenegrin, she had heard that there were a lot of people from Montenegro there, although she had no idea where to find Montenegro on the map.

However, one day, when she mentioned the name to Laureano, he burst out laughing.

Alegna d'Ortsac? It was simply Ângela Castro spelled backwards. Hadn't she realised?

She almost wept with rage, and from then on, she removed Alegna from any future plans. 'Alegna is a LIE,' she wrote in red pencil on the advice columns she had collected. She felt violated, mocked. Alegna didn't even exist, but she had made her dream.

Only later did he go into the kitchen, open the fridge and take a beer, a glass and the opener back with him into the living room, where he put them down on the table beside the sofa and then slowly drank the beer, looking straight ahead.

In the painting, the black woman was moving away, with her back to him, carrying a can of water on her head and holding her child by the hand. Two thin, isolated figures trudging up the hill that disappeared into the jungle beyond. They had walked many miles to fetch that can of water, he thought. He had known the real-life versions of those lanky silhouettes carrying water on their head, women who walked vast distances barefoot, figures barely sketched in, as if they were dissolving into the earth.

A can of water, almost every drop of which would be eked out, to be drunk or added to flour. He knew how much sweat a can of water cost.

He had once met a woman who had called her son Sofrimento – Suffering. A small black boy called Sofrimento Nassiaaca.

'Cummeroysh' and 'luggoshteensh' said the pronunciation guides for tourists, to make life easier for the foreigners who sought out the shops with signs saying 'English Spoken' or 'Afrikaans Gesprek'.

She was drawn to languages, as she was to all things foreign. One day she had carefully copied into a notebook two sentences found in a couple of leaflets. The first was about John Orr: 'The finest department store in the city, with merchandise from every country in the world. Twenty departments and separate rest-, writing- and powder-rooms, for the use of customers only.'

The second was about Casa Hofali, 'the Perfume Shop. All the best-known French perfumes, and a varied assortment of cosmetics from the beauty centres of the world.' She didn't understand what they meant, but felt that each sentence was communicating something superlative, possibly exceptional. Hofali?

A few days later, she found herself in Praça Sete de Março. It was a hot October day, but there was a breeze.

Here and there in the almost clear sky floated thin white clouds.

She passed the Standard Bank, went into the Prédio Fonte Azul and, for the first time, walked through the doors of Casa Hofali.

When she stood before the glass display cases of gloves, handbags, jewellery and perfumes, she felt immediately that this was a very refined shop. There was a particular aroma in the air, all-pervading and yet almost imperceptible.

As she looked about her, something inside her said that, in a way, the Casa Hofali sold only the inessential things of life. You could live without jewellery or perfume. In that climate, gloves and furs were quite superfluous, a luxury that could only be shown off on very rare occasions. But that was precisely what attracted her, it was why she had gone into that shop. She wanted the superfluous, the luxurious, what was reserved for the few.

She put her handbag down on the counter and faced the assistant.

Did she wish to see gloves or perhaps jewellery? A new collection of French jewellery had just come in. What could he show her?

'Perfumes,' she said, without hesitation and taking a deep breath.

'Any perfume in particular?'

She glanced at the variously shaped bottles, each beside its respective box. They were too far away for her to be able to read the names. She remembered having seen 'Tabu' in Dora Flávia's bathroom. And what were those others, the many others, already open, that Dora kept on the marble shelf in front of the mirror? She couldn't think of a single name and felt mildly embarrassed. She hadn't prepared properly for this visit.

'I definitely don't want "Tabu",' she said with a boldness bordering on aggression. 'It's a present for someone,' she added in more measured tones, 'so it has to suit her personality. Perhaps you could show me a few others.'

'Of course,' he said, placing on the counter 'Sirocco', 'Elle', 'Orage', 'Madeiras do Oriente', 'Promessa', 'Embrujo de Sevilla'. He always brought both the original bottle and another fitted with an atomiser, with which he lightly sprayed the inside of her wrist, near her watchstrap. She savoured each one, but always rejected them. She put the bottles down on the counter again, silently admired their whimsical shapes, the perfection of their glass stoppers, which resembled jewels, especially one that was topped off by a small black cut-glass ball.

'No, it's not quite right.'

'Is it for a young lady?'

He was pleasant and solicitous, had slender hands and wore slightly tinted glasses. He seemed prepared to spend all morning serving her. He offered her a chair, which she accepted with an unexpected feeling of well-being, finding relief from a weariness which, curiously, she had only just realised she felt.

'Yes, for a young lady,' she said, breathing in another perfume and aware for a moment of the noise of the city outside. 'Tall and blonde.' Then she added after a brief pause: 'And foreign.'

(A rich woman, who has everything she could possibly want, she thought, leaning back and resting her hands on the arms of the chair. A pretty woman, surrounded by admirers.)

'We have "Madame Rochas",' he said. 'Or "Femme" by Marcel Rochas. Perfume or eau de toilette?'

'Rochas is a Portuguese name, isn't it?' she said, annoyed because he had pronounced it as if it were.

No, no, he was quick to assure her, it was definitely French, as was the perfume. She need only look at the box.

In the end, she chose a different one – an eau de toilette – seduced as much by the smell as by the unusual design on the box. It was, she thought, a heavy, almost extravagant perfume, but she was quite sure about her choice.

'You might not think it suitable for a young lady,' the assistant said in silken tones, 'but she may have just the right personality for it.' Some girls of eighteen bought that very perfume and, besides, age was irrelevant really, wasn't it, it was all a question of taste? A very personal matter.

She watched him carefully wrap it up, as if it were a jewel, enfolding the box in what seemed to her a sumptuous sheet of glossy paper, then he meticulously finished it off with a label and some gold thread.

She walked across Praça Sete de Março and resisted the temptation to unwrap the package right there, then open the bottle and succumb to the perfume's seductive smell. It was a gift to herself; she deserved some expensive perfume, too expensive, it's true, but she had paid for it with her own money, Amélia Capítulo's money, earned by the work of her own hands.

Amélia Capítulo. Lord, how she hated that name. Not Amélia, which had even been the name of a queen, the last queen of Portugal, and was the name of that other city, Porto Amélia – but she didn't want to think about all that, it was forgotten, left behind.

Amélia was her name, and she liked it. But Capítulo was just impossible, how could anyone be called Capítulo? She never mentioned it in Dora Flávia's house. She was known there only as Amélia.

However, although she didn't dislike the name Amélia, it wouldn't have been her choice. It had been chosen by her godmother, and for that reason alone, she wished she could set it aside and never use it again. If she could choose, she would rather be, say, Patrícia, which was the name both of a street and of a princess – Avenida Princesa Patrícia. Patrícia what, though, if she were to have a name she really liked?

Patrícia Hart. A tall, blonde woman. A foreigner. A pretty, rich, much-admired woman. Patrícia Hart.

She took her place automatically, absent-mindedly, in the queue for the bus and slowly unwrapped the package while she waited, unaware of the eyes of the other people watching her with interest. She carefully removed the stopper, placed a drop of perfume on the inside of her wrist and breathed in the aroma, again and again, focused solely on that. Yes, she thought, it would suit Patrícia Hart.

Sofrimento Nassiaaca. He knew and had seen how the Black people suffered, he knew it from the inside, he could put himself in their place, because he didn't feel and never had felt any distance from them. He was no different.

He remembered the earth being scattered over the coffin of Relito Matunga's father, at the back of the cemetery, where there were no graves with statues of angels holding hourglasses, marble plaques or candelabra. In the place where the poor Whites and Blacks were laid to rest. That, he thought, is where he would end up one day. He would feel fine there, next to the Blacks. At peace.

She enjoyed lying to them. She didn't know why. She felt better like that, hiding her thoughts from them, just as she concealed from them her solitary Sunday walks.

She needed that – to be alone, to stroll by the sea, across the square paving stones, past the tall, straight coconut palms and the stone balustrades – two straight lines that seemed to meet on the horizon. (But wasn't the point where they met also the point from which they were fleeing?)

The dishevelled palm trees, always swaying in the wind. Some had a broad white stripe painted on the trunk and revealed, now and then, scorched yellow leaves. Where they were rooted in the earth, the trunk was wider and fatter, rougher and darker in colour, like the leg of an elephant. But above that, higher up, the trunks were so slender, like thin lines, seemingly getting thinner as they grew taller, the rows of trees continuing as far as the horizon. And the sea beside her was also in flight, setting off on the waves for Xefina,

Inhaca, Bazaruto, for other countries, other ports, other islands.

She liked walking past the coconut trees, her hair ruffled by the wind, she liked that Sunday afternoon breeze that blew her hair back from her face and emptied her head of dreams.

Whereas the others, the vampires who had sucked the blood from the Blacks, would emerge one day from their lavish tombs, wherever they were, and like the living dead would wander among the gravestones, finding neither rest nor sleep.

He would not be among them, though. He would be lying at peace in an ordinary grave among the Blacks. With only a little earth on top of him, so that he could hear the birds singing.

Walking without feeling or thinking anything. Walking over the slender, shifting shadows of the coconut palms. Hearing her heels tap-tapping on the paving stones, as if her feet belonged to someone else.

And then she would run for the bus, rush home, change her clothes, and sit down mechanically at her sewing-machine, her thoughts elsewhere, as if she were sleeping with her eyes wide open, glad that Gita kept Laureano busy and filled the long Sunday hours.

They would finally arrive, always after she did. They would tell her things, and she would say yes, yes, pretending to listen and even asking questions, whose answers she would ignore, thinking about the next Sunday. About the streets she had walked along and of which they knew nothing. She heard them talking above the constant noise of the sewing-machine, monotonous as the sound of the waves. Or the wind.

The needle always ran forwards over the cloth, always forwards, like a mad thing. The cloth was as huge, as vast as the sea, and there were no shores, she was pedalling furiously because her feet had broken free and no longer obeyed her, she was the needle rushing ever onwards – or so she had dreamed once. It was an old, forgotten dream. But now it came back into her mind, the idea that she was the needle, a mad needle stitching furiously away at the sea.

Until he was more established, he'd had only passing affairs with women, Black and White, but never anything serious. He didn't want to be tied down. Marriage was a nice idea, but brought with it a lot of responsibilities. At the end of each month, even when he cut down on cigarettes, he never had any money left in the drawer. And now and then, he still sent some home to his mother and to Narciso.

A mad needle stitching furiously away at the sea – ah, dreams. Foolish, random thoughts that drifted through your head while you were sleeping. She was back in her godmother's house and they were mourning the recent death of someone or other. And yet despite this, they had thrown a party and there was dancing out on the terrace and the sound of music, then suddenly the man she was dancing with was carrying her off somewhere and embracing her in the middle of a field, and she felt the weight of his body on hers, felt that he loved her and that they would shortly run away together, but in the dream she also knew that none of this was possible. She had woken up feeling breathless and bathed in sweat.

The little secrets she kept hidden, for no reason, simply because she liked to keep part of her life to herself, even if they were silly, useless things, like the advertisements she cut out of newspapers.

However absurd, she enjoyed reading them and found them fascinating. Say nine Hail Marys each day for nine days and make three wishes: one wish to do with business and two impossible wishes. On the ninth day publish this advertisement and your wishes will all come true even if you don't believe it.

Prayer to Our Lord of the Heavy-Laden. Prayer for those in distress: The Virgin knelt in distress at the foot of the cross, see my distress O Mother of Jesus. Publish this on the third day and wait to see what happens on the fourth.

Prayer to St Onuphrius: O Glorious St Onuphrius who climbed Mount Tabor and clothed yourself in green leaves.

Gentleman newly arrived from Portugal seeks lodgings; maintenance fitter seeks suitable employment; honest gentleman seeks — goodness, how foolish to believe in these stories about honest gentlemen and marriages made at a distance.

Zuze, Medium, Clairvoyant, Spiritualist and Scientist, Master of the Absolute Powers. Resolves problems however difficult or impossible in fifteen days. Success guaranteed. Instantly brings lovers together or drives them apart. If you want to start a new life, waste no time, contact Professor Doctor Master Zuze.

To spend all afternoon walking in the Baixa (and then tell them calmly over supper that she'd only popped out for a quarter of an hour to buy buttons from the corner shop), to walk along hearing the sound of her high heels on the ground, seeing her shadow running along the pavement beside her, slender, elastic, a very agile shadow that was only there in passing and sometimes disappeared through a doorway, got lost in the tangle of traffic, in the profusion of objects available in a large department store like John Orr's for example.

She loved John Orr's, its glass façade and the whole imposing building that took up all of one block and had entrances in various streets. Inside lay an abundance of things on display, one section after another, furniture, home furnishings, bed linen, underwear, menswear, womenswear and children's clothing, shoes, luggage, toys. And because it was December, they were handing out free Coca-Cola, and kids were having their photograph taken with men dressed up as Father Christmas.

Please don't let them invite her, dear God, please don't let them invite her to go to Sakarbai Lalá's house or Relito's house, or to a picnic on the beach with André, Jamal and Bibila. She wanted to spend the afternoon alone, going up and down to the different departments in John Orr's, rubbing shoulders with the customers who came and went, pushing her way past them, looking but seeing only a confused glow, hearing children's voices and laughter as if they were talking and laughing somewhere far away.

As if nothing were real, as if she were caught up in a scene where she was enjoyably lost, dazed by the sound of voices, dazzled by the bright blinking lights.

To get lost just for a moment, because she always had to go back home in the end and pretend to enjoy the nuts and dried fruit bought at Prodag and the improvised Christmas tree balanced precariously on the kitchen bench, and to swoon over the gift she would unwrap that night – a scarf made from artificial silk or a pair of shoes that she would have had to buy anyway.

No, please don't let them invite her, dear God, don't ever let them invite her to go to the Zoo to see the clowns Emiliano and Vosnes, or to listen to the band in the Jardim Vasco da Gama on a Sunday afternoon.

When she left John Orr's, she would go and sit down at a table in the Continental or the Scala and slowly read a magazine, then order coffee and cake (she always chose *pastéis de nata*, which she had once heard someone on the next table refer to as 'custard tarts').

She would sit down in the Continental or the Scala, savouring that small round tart with the creamy filling, burnt on top, and taking small sips not of coffee, which she had decided would be too intense and too dark, but a cup of strong tea to which she would add a little milk or a few drops of lemon juice. Then she would signal to the waiter, glance at the bill, pay without saying a word, as if she neither understood nor spoke Portuguese, leave a tip on the tray and then leave, her hair swinging and her handbag over her shoulder.

And when she crossed the street by the pedestrian crossing and passed by Lopes & Ramos, she would perhaps remember having seen in the paper the advertisement for the sunset dance being held that night in the Chez Mona Club at the Hotel Girassol, and the Rendez-vous Coty in the reception rooms of the Hotel Polana, sponsored by shops such as Costa & Cordeiro, Coimbra, Fabião, as well as Lopes & Ramos and John Orr of course.

She would perhaps remember those advertisements along with the other mysterious ads she read in the paper, in which people played with fate as if they were fire-eaters or were swinging back and forth on a trapeze high above, hanging by one foot, risking their lives.

He whistled as he walked along beneath the trees of Xipamanine, past the boys unloading shirts, caps, plastic bowls and bath towels, and the sellers of spells and fetishes sitting on sacks, upturned buckets or small wooden stools.

The women wore headscarves, skirts and blouses, or *capulanas* tied about their waists; the scarves, *capulanas* and blouses all had different patterns, and the rule (if there had to be a rule, although why should there) was that everything went with everything else, so that any combination was possible, and the results were surprising. He saw the blend of colours, especially if he looked not just at one woman, but at a group of two or more, for they usually walked in groups. They were like a living, moving painting.

Yes, it could have been Dora Flávia's husband, the engineer, waiting for her on the quay. Her life had missed being entirely different by a mere fluke, a stroke of fate, a nothing – a dice that falls showing one face and not another, a roulette wheel that spins for just a moment longer and stops on the next number.

She had passed the engineer on the stairs and was so struck by the thought that it could have been him that day waiting for her on the quay, that she stumbled and fell. He rushed to her aid, took her hand and very nearly picked her up, helping her onto the chaise longue in the corridor.

'Are you all right?' he asked, smiling. He asked other questions too, offered her a cup of coffee, ordered Zélia to go and fetch her a glass of water.

'No, it's nothing,' she assured him. She had twisted her foot slightly, that was all, it wasn't anything serious.

'Irmantino will take you home,' he said, looking concerned or at least pretending to be. 'Is it very painful?'

She shook her head, but her eyes filled with tears.

'It obviously is,' he said and told Zélia to summon Irmantino and, on the way, to bring some tablets from the bathroom – the ones in the blue box with a stripe down the middle. In the bathroom cabinet.

That was how she came to be driven home in the engineer's car, and she continued to lie about her injury when she got there. Yes, she had twisted her foot, it had hurt terribly, she'd never known such pain. She didn't even feel like talking and wouldn't come down to supper because she couldn't swallow. Would they please just leave her alone in her room in the dark, with a cold compress on her forehead.

And yet what a glory and a joy it had been to cross the city in the engineer's car, sitting on the right-hand side in the back seat, almost lying down because she had taken off her shoe and was resting her foot on the beige upholstery, which smelled of leather.

The cool air-conditioned air was blowing on her face, she felt lighter, and deep down inside, experienced an obscure sense of relief. Without turning around, but looking at her in the rear-view mirror, Irmantino made some remark or other, which she later forgot, but it had made her smile at the time, and he laughed too, his shoulders shaking and his cap jiggling about on his head.

The city seemed different, loftier and more distant seen through the car's windows, especially through the broad windscreen with its band of darkened glass along the top. The acacias swayed and their red flowers appeared to bend down to greet her before being rapidly left behind.

And then there was the pleasure of waiting, sitting in the car, clutching her handbag, while Irmantino got out, walked round and opened the door for her.

And all of this was seen, studied and observed by the neighbours who were, she was sure, peeping out from behind their curtains.

Africa was full of every possible design and every possible colour – plains and mountains, rivers and scrubland, waterfalls and jungles, sea and savannah, reptiles and antelopes, elephants and birds, flowers and fruit.

He would enjoy acting as guide to the woman who was about to arrive.

The Hotel Polana was a vast luminous façade, all in white. She had noticed, when walking past, strolling slowly along Rua Bayly, that the curtains at the windows were white too, but perhaps that was just the lining or only one side of them. Seen from within, they might, in fact, be made of a large floral print. Not that she would ever know, since she had never been in one of the bedrooms.

She had, of course, visited the hotel, although she had only seen the great atrium with its plush lifts, whose doors would suddenly slide open to let someone out, and the front reception room with its marble floor and gilt tables on which there were vast arrangements of strelitzias and anturias. And she had been through the next door too, which gave onto the garden, the swimming-pool and the sea.

The landscape suddenly flooded your eyes, presenting a boundless vista, as if the sea were part of the garden, lying just beyond the flower beds, the small green squares of lawn, the interlaced white-and-grey paving stones. Below, when you went down the steps and reached the wooden balustrade, the sea stretched away for as far as you could see.

It wasn't really very different from the view she could see from the street. An oil tanker was passing in the distance, there were sailing boats and white-capped waves. The coconut palms along the coast were more sparsely grouped — just a few isolated trees here and there, all bent in the same direction by the wind.

But there were palm trees in the hotel garden too, and if you turned your back on the coast, you could see how they rose up in the middle of the lawn, encircling the intensely blue water of the swimming pool. And from that same view-point, you couldn't help but notice how that side of the hotel was full of windows, balconies, columns and balustrades, letting in sun and sea, and how this more protected and sheltered side (like the garden itself), was in a way the most important, as if the part of the hotel that faced onto the street was merely a façade, behind which the true reality lay hidden.

This protected side was only for the few, for those who sat on their balconies on white chairs at white tables or reclined on the blue sunbeds beneath the parasols beside the pool, while uniformed waiters passed noiselessly among them, bearing trays.

That side did not belong to her. She was merely a visitor and was permitted a rapid, almost furtive glance around. At some point, she would always come up against the gilt signs informing her that the swimming pool was reserved for hotel guests only. As were the garden, the beauty of it all, the calm evening, the reception rooms, the dining tables and the music at the dances held at night. Life, yes, even life did not belong to her.

She had completely forgotten about Joaquim Albano, she thought, as she walked past the hotel, where a large, gleaming car had just driven in.

She wouldn't have wanted to stay in the village and live her life, as Adelina did, between the grocery store, the vegetable plot and the street. She really wouldn't. She had no regrets. Joaquim was a lost memory, dead and forgotten. He no longer existed.

(The uniformed porter was holding the door open for the man and woman getting out of the car. The woman took a few steps towards the hotel, while one hotel employee took the suitcases and another placed them on a trolley. The man closed the car door and with a few quick strides joined the woman who was waiting for him at the entrance to the hotel. When he closed the boot, Amélia heard a tiny metallic click.)

When she thought about Joaquim, all she felt was anger. When he insisted on sleeping with her, she should, as she realised later, simply have played hard to get. She should have said, No, sir, not until we're married. And that was why he went after Adelina, who was such a sly little thing and so guarded, Adelina, who would receive that fine grocery store as a dowry, whereas she would get nothing.

But it had probably been because of the things his mother and her godmother had said, because mothers only got involved in other people's lives in order to ruin them. And his mother was very pleased for him to marry Adelina.

And then her wretched godmother had realised what those stones thrown up at her window meant and had beaten her about the head with an umbrella. (Somewhere in the world the broken pieces of that umbrella must still exist.)

Oh, she would make her pay for that when she swept into the village one day in a shiny car, wearing a fur coat and gold necklaces and bracelets. And she would return her godfather's gold watch to Palmira, as if it were so much trash that she was throwing in her face.

He wrote to her that night when he got back from Xipamanine. (As he passed an old woman sitting crouched on a mat, she had held out to him a little wooden doll, about the size of his finger. 'Buy it for her,' she said. 'So she'll have children.') He didn't tell Amélia about that. He talked to her about the scrubland, the plantations, the citrus trees, the swamps, the hunting.

And he promised that he would sometimes take her out to supper. He had a friend who owned a restaurant and whose wife did the cooking, chicken piri-piri or à *cafreal* as they called it. The place was always full, and on Sundays, it was every man for himself, because there simply wasn't room for the number of people queuing at the door. But they always managed to find a table for friends.

She had defended herself as best she could, trying to escape, covering her head with her hands and arms, but her god-mother only beat her all the harder, thrashed her with the umbrella as if it were a cane. She heard it whistle through the air around her head before she felt the pain, then she fell, her ears bleeding, and the broken umbrella flew into the air – yes, somewhere in the world the broken pieces of that umbrella must still exist.

'Like mother like daughter,' said Marta and Rosa, as they did their laundry at the village wash-house. 'Blood will out.'

And Alice would nod and continue pounding the clothes. 'Yes, no two ways about it, she's just like her mother.'

Her godmother was making her a paper boat and putting her inside it (now that you've been dishonoured, no man is going to want you, my girl). She was as small as a tin soldier and the sodden boat floated unsteadily down the gutter.

You asked for a crumb, and God, if he chose, would give you food in abundance. That was what the Blacks did, and so he did the same. He imitated them because they knew about these things. He asked life for a little happiness, the size of an ant's leg, and life would give him happiness in abundance.

135

Everything seemed to have gone much better for him since he had been carrying that woman's photo around in his wallet.

He went out at night with his best friends, Relito Matunga, Tito Umbina, Jamal Uamusse and André Naene. They tended not to go to the bars in Araújo, which were favoured by the bourgeoisie and the tourists, they went elsewhere, to dance the real African dances. But that night, which for him was almost his last as a bachelor, they had decided to go to Araújo.

'Oh, the Street of Sin,' they sang at four in the morning, staggering along the road, their arms about each other.

The passage of time. Like a pulled thread, like a needle running. Month after month, year after year, Sunday after Sunday.

Alone in the empty house, she sighed and went into the kitchen, where she poured boiling water over the coffee that was delivered direct to the house (she dialled 4164 and ordered it over the phone, never tiring of the pleasure she felt at that prompt service).

Without her realising it, life was slipping by. It seemed impossible, but several years had passed.

When he opened the envelope and looked at the photo, he knew that she was the one, however many other women might write to him.

'She's gorgeous,' he thought. She had big, bright eyes, which he would like to see in real life or in a colour photo, wavy hair held back with a slide on either side, and she looked so serene in that white blouse with the lace-trimmed collar. Only her smile seemed a little sad.

Several years, but nothing ever happened. Never. She understood those attacks of Licínio's now, his bouts of 'phylloxera' that sent him hurtling off down the roads in the heat and the dust. She didn't like him, but she understood the feeling.

Dear Reader, evil exists and its cure lies so close to hand that it either cannot be seen or evil itself will not let it be seen. Even a problem that is a problem for many people can be resolved simply by consulting Mamana Muéra, the Great Astrologer and Internationally Renowned Shaman. Discover the origin of your failures, past, present and future. Problems of love, envy, the evil eye. Aura-cleansing every Monday. Considered to be one of the best Astrologers. Payment on results. Personal consultations and at a distance.

Portuguese gentleman, resident in Sydney, has car, own house, flourishing business, would like to meet lady, 28–38, for correspondence by letter, with a possible view to matrimony. Bob Pereira, P.O. Box . . . Sydney.

Great new offers from Café Cazumbi. Do you suffer with your stomach? Try our famous Ogard tea. On sale at the Centro Ervanário de Moçambique.

Where was Sydney? She put down the newspaper and promptly forgot the name, but it came back into her head that night when she forgot to take the herbal tea that helped her sleep.

She switched on Gita's globe and ran her index finger across its illuminated surface. At last, she found it – in Australia, good God, Sydney was in Australia. A vast country that you could, it seemed, reach by following a straight line. Except, of course, there was a sea in between.

She sighed, positioning the globe more securely on the narrow sewing-machine cover. Everything was so far away when there was a sea to be crossed.

Australia had kangaroos, that was all she knew. If she wrote to him – not that she would write, why would she? – if she wrote to him it would be to ask if there were kangaroos in Sydney too.

Bob Pereira said that there weren't (for she had written to him after all), he sent her a picture postcard of Sydney and another, also in colour, a shot of a kangaroo leaping almost as high as the tree beside it, or so it seemed, with its small front legs, its pointed ears and its long snout like a mountain goat's – or so it seemed.

What did Sydney remind her of? Of Capetown, she decided, the city with the skyscrapers that she never got to see.

She put both postcards away in the drawer and forgot about them because it was as if they weren't real and she had never received them.

But she was intrigued by that experience of going to collect letters from the poste restante, as if they had nothing to do with her and she had suddenly leapt into someone else's life.

And because she liked secrets and took pleasure in lying, she lied to Bob Pereira too. He would never know her real address or her real name. She signed herself Patrícia Hart, as if another person were doing the writing and she merely served as an intermediary, collecting mail that did not belong to her.

She felt nervous every time she went into the post office, as if there were something shameful and illicit about going to collect letters from a poste restante. It took ages for her to get up the nerve to go in and she would stand out in the street, looking across at the blue-painted building, as if its peaceful, symmetrical appearance might calm her or as if she wanted to memorise the stone steps, the round arches edged with a white frieze, the ornate balcony above.

She hesitated before finally gathering enough courage together to cross the road and go up the steps, heart pounding.

Inside was a gleaming, spacious area supported on pillars. Light poured in through the glass roof in the middle, and all around the upper floor was a wrought-iron balustrade, painted white, with a repeated geometric design that resembled an open fan or a peacock's tail. Behind the balustrade, in the corners, were potted plants.

She had noticed all these things only gradually, letter after letter, while she waited in the queue at the counter, always hoping that it would be a different clerk from the one who had dealt with her before. However, things almost never worked out as she wanted, even though she made a special effort to come at different times and on different days, for it was usually the same bespectacled mulatto woman who would peer at her for a moment and check the address against her identity card: Miss Patrícia Hart. And below that, in smaller writing: c/o Amélia S. Marcelino Capítulo.

This proved complicated the first time because the woman said that she could only give the letter to Patrícia Hart herself. She couldn't come, Amélia said. She'd had an accident. She was ill, very ill indeed. She had almost died. A car accident. Yes, that was it. But she was there, in person, Amélia S. (for dos Santos) Marcelino Capítulo, just like the name and photo on the identity card. After all, that was the other name on the envelope, wasn't it?

The woman hesitated, turned the letter over as if in search of some further clue, adjusted her glasses, and looked at her inquisitorially for a moment, in silence.

Finally, she shrugged and handed her the envelope. Amélia noticed that her nail varnish was cracked.

On the other hand, Amélia thought, as she went out through the door and down the steps of the arcade again (she counted them for the first time, there were five), meeting the same clerk over and over made things easier because she didn't have to keep explaining the situation. Sometimes, though, the clerk would smile an almost familiar smile as she handed her the letter – once again pointlessly checking the name against her identity card – and ask how Patrícia Hart was getting on.

'She's a little better, thank you,' Amélia would say, retrieving her identity card and hurriedly leaving. Goodness, common people always had such a horrible habit of trying to strike up a conversation, everyone spoke to everyone else, as if talking about your own life were the most natural thing in the world.

Then she would go and sit in the Continental or the Scala or, if she happened to catch a bus without having to wait too long, in the Café Dominó. She drank her tea with milk or lemon as she read the letter, then leafed slowly through a fashion magazine, choosing the dresses she would have her couturier make – if she were Patrícia Hart.

The passage of time. Like a pulled thread, year after year, day after day, Sunday after Sunday.

When she looked at old photographs now, it was almost as if they were different people. (The marriage by proxy, with Uncle Alfredo standing in for the groom because the advertisement had been found wrapped around his shoes. They had all laughed and drunk champagne. She had quickly downed another glass after emptying the first.)

As if they were different people. Laureano, Gita, herself. Some things were growing ever more remote, for example, that business with the ballet lessons, how long ago that seemed. Only yesterday Gita had been a little girl and suddenly she was halfway through secondary school, goodness, how time passed, and if it weren't for Palette Colour Shampoo, she herself would doubtless have a few grey hairs.

Sunday after Sunday, month after month, and now it was fifteen years since she first arrived.

He bought a different shaving lotion, new shoes and new clothes, placed a vase of flowers in the bedroom, a bottle of champagne in the fridge and a basket of fruit in the kitchen.

He counted off the weeks on the calendar. Time seemed to move so slowly, and then suddenly, there it was. The big day. He looked at the clock yet again. It was time to leave the house, go down to the Baixa and hurry to the quay.

The streets were heaving with people, as if the whole city were hurrying down to the quay, as if going to meet the ship were still, as it used to be, a kind of holiday, an extra Sunday, a saint's day or a religious festival.

The city was in festive mood and yet it had no idea that he was expecting his wife, that they were already man and wife, even though they had never met, the city had no idea what it was that moved him and left a lump in his throat.

By now, he thought, as he paced back and forth on the quay, looking at his watch and cleaning his glasses, which kept misting up with the heat, the sweat and the excitement, by now, she would be standing on the deck of the approaching ship.

But she didn't want to arrive, she really didn't. As the ship approached port, she locked herself in the bathroom, looking in the mirror and applying make-up and more make-up.

She would have been up on deck from early on. She would see Ponta Vermelha first and the tall Towers, and then, just when she'd begun to think that the ship had lost its way, the city would suddenly appear out of nowhere, because that was how it was, you sailed on and on across the sea until you came in sight of the coast, and then, after you had passed one island and another, a black line appeared on the horizon, which gradually became tinged with green and white – beyond lay the *planalto*, the tableland, and you began to see houses up above and others at the foot, like tiny settlements or scattered villages, and then you rounded Ponta Vermelha and the hidden city suddenly appeared, out of nowhere.

She didn't want to arrive, she really didn't.

Still locked in the bathroom, she decided that she would let everyone else get off first, Orlanda's parents, the nuns, the people in the cabin next to hers, the other passengers she didn't know. To gain time. She would say that she'd just wanted to make herself look pretty. Standing at the mirror, applying make-up and more make-up.

And so she didn't realise that they were in sight of the coast, that they were passing one island and then another, she didn't see that line on the horizon that gradually became tinged with green and white, didn't see the *planalto* or the tall Towers nor, as they rounded Ponta Vermelha, did she see the white city suddenly appear out of nowhere.

Only afterwards, when the ship had been moored for some time and all the noise and confusion on board caused by the other people disembarking had died down – the voices, the shouts, the clatter of feet, the sound of luggage being dragged along – only then did he finally see her, standing at the top of the stairs, with a small trunk at her side.

3

The first lover was the sun, prowling around when you lay on the sand, licking you with its tongue, flicking you with its tail, sniffing with its snout of light – you could see this through your eyelids, with no need to open your eyes, while your body grew soft and the smell of the wind grew stronger – and then the sun began to take over your body, advancing with cautious steps, like a wild beast, and you surrendered, yielded, and the sun entered through skin, ears, nostrils, mouth, and there came a moment when you abandoned all resistance and opened your legs and received the sun in the very centre of your body – the sun, yes, the sun was your first lover.

Or the sea, perhaps the sea was your first lover, when you lay down on the sand, very still, barely breathing, tense with expectation, and it rose up noiselessly from afar and suddenly burst over you, flooding you with its foaming drool.

As I lie on the beach with Rodrigo's hand resting on mine, it occurs to me that falling in love is a very accurate way of describing the experience – you do *fall* in love. We're all lying on the beach, Ditinha, Titita, Joana, Ramesh Kumar, Ibrahim and Zaida, Jussa, Roberto Crisântemo, Júlio, whom we always called Juliô, with the stress on the final syllable, Joaquim Barata, Valentina Ueja, João Saiote, Micas Julai, Carolina Matimele, Nuno Varela, Tójó, Juvenal, Alberta, me and Rodrigo. We are all still together this summer. And again I think, yes, falling in love.

'Get out of there!' shouts Juliô, sitting up on his towel and throwing a pebble at a dog sticking its nose into the various baskets containing our lunch. 'Bloody dog!' he shouts again, waving his arms and running towards him. But the dog won't be shooed away, it merely trots a short way off, then lies down on the sand, stubborn and expectant. Two other dogs approach, sniffing, ears drooping, and lie down, noses on paws, at a respectful distance from the first.

Juliô gives up and merely drags our beach bags and baskets closer to where we're lying. 'Hey, you,' he shouts, turning to us, 'The next time I'm not going to see them off, all right? So keep a watchful eye on those guys over there.'

'It's hot,' says Joana, getting up. 'Anyone fancy a dip?'

No one does, and she goes off alone, a small figure in a dark swimsuit running down to the water, where she plunges in, and then all you can see is a head moving along on the surface.

'Let's go to the club tonight,' says Titita. 'Anyone who doesn't will have to buy everyone else a drink tomorrow.'

Dancing at the club, with the lights gyrating madly on the ceiling. Suddenly, a curtain would open at the far end, and the sea would appear, fringed with foam. And the lights travelled round the room, occasionally touching my shoulder, on which a man's hand was resting.

The thin straps holding up my dress hurt my skin, burned from the sun. I didn't feel the pain, though, aware only of that hand running down my back, touching each vertebra, from neck to waist. His other hand was holding mine, tensely, tightly. Sometimes trembling a little. Further off were our feet on the gleaming dance-floor almost filled by other couples turning and circling.

And there was that feeling of being alive, intensely alive, the sense that this was a high point in one's life. We wanted to be there and live the moment because the next moment everything might vanish and nothing would be the same – everything might pass, like clothes and fashions, and the summer would suddenly be gone.

We were afraid that the world, or life, would end because in Africa everything happened so abruptly – night falling, fruit ripening, people leaving. We were afraid of death, even though our bodies told us we were immortal. Childhood had come to an abrupt close − life grew like a tree and up there where the branches spread out, a part of life was over.

Yet this wasn't a sad idea, there was no room for sadness then: there was a wave that picked us up, drove us out of the school corridors and playgrounds and propelled us towards the beach; something took us over, like Licínio's attacks of 'phylloxera', or even stronger than that. But without Licínio's melancholy.

Life was approaching, you could feel its light step nearby, but it wasn't frightening. You stood before the mirror and adjusted a hairslide or touched up your lipstick, you drank chilled wine and knew that life, too, was to be drunk like wine, and was equally intoxicating. It was passing through us, you knew this when you were dancing, looking out at the lights beyond, perhaps the lights of ships far off on the horizon. It brought the certainty of a lover, the real one this time, because the time came when your first lover wasn't the sun or the sea, but a man.

You had always known this, it was written on your body, in your blood, on the palms of your hand. You would be standing at the mirror, brushing your hair and you knew that everything had begun a long time ago.

Just a few months earlier, I was thinking: 'I'll be seventeen this summer.'

The new season was a long way off then and the air at night was still cool. Suddenly, though, the sky had changed, the city had changed, the shopwindows were full of new clothes, as well as china, lace, dresses and embroidered tablecloths.

I notice, as I walk past every day on the way to school, that the houses have their windows open − I wonder if they are bedrooms, the ones with balconies and in which you can occasionally see figures moving about. I imagine lovers in hotel rooms with the curtains drawn shut.

'Are we going to eat or not?' says Ramesh, standing up. 'I don't know about you, but I'm starving.'

'You would be,' says Alberta, and everyone bursts out laughing because fat Ramesh is always hungry and likes to describe his night raids on the fridge and how he trips over the big coconut grater in the dark. He knows the grater is always there in the same place and swears he'll avoid it, but he only remembers this when it's too late and he's already knocked it over and woken up the whole household. His father rants and raves upstairs, his brother calls him a donkey and a loon, he himself beats the wall and rages at the wretched grater, but the following night he does exactly the same.

'He's a real menace when it comes to lunch,' laughs Carolina, running over to the baskets.

'He's worse than marabunta ants,' says Roberto springing to his feet. 'If you get there too late, there'll be nothing left.'

In an instant, the baskets and the beach bags are almost empty, and they had seemed so heavy when we carried them onto the ferry.

The ferry, this morning. Rushing along, carrying everything, out of breath, because if we missed it, we would have to wait half an hour or more, and we didn't want to do that. We all piled on at the last minute.

'Why is it we never arrive anywhere on time?' asks Ditinha. But no one is listening, we're all talking louder and louder and laughing in a superior way, as if the ferry could never possibly have left without us.

There are no benches, and so we lean on the rail or sit on the coils of ropes or on the steps. The ferry is packed, there are people everywhere, mostly standing, although others are sitting on the floor, on crates or upturned buckets. A beer bottle gets knocked over and the liquid runs towards us, forming a thick, foaming trail.

'Hey, someone must have peed himself,' says Juvenal. 'It was Joaquim, Nuno, Tójó,' we all shout, and laugh even louder and jostle each other.

148

A little black albino boy stares at us in alarm. His eyes are inflamed, the lids almost stuck together and very red.

Two hunters get out of a jeep and start talking, leaning against the doors. One of them is drunk and begins insulting a man in a car, while the other hunter tries to shut him up and finally succeeds, almost by force. Stuck inside the jeep, the dogs are growing impatient and appear at the windows, barking.

Up ahead, some sports fishermen are also getting out of their car; one of them lights a cigarette, then returns both lighter and cigarette pack to his shirt pocket. Seagulls come and go, some move off towards the quay, where you can see their wings silhouetted against the light. Below, to the right, big ships are moored and you can read their names from here. But I don't bother, it's the city I want to look at, until we reach Ponta Vermelha: the Girassol, the Towers, the roof of the station, the cathedral, the tall buildings, cranes, warehouses, the white, luminous outline of the houses, while ahead lies the waveless sea, the colour of lead.

On the ferry back, at the end of the day, there will be women carrying great buckets of giant prawns to sell in the city; they wait impatiently for the ferry to dock and then race off, carrying their buckets, because whoever arrives first sells first – the rush to leave, footsteps echoing down the quay.

There's a rush to leave now too. We've reached Catembe and people are in a hurry, as are the jeeps and cars, and the ferry soon empties. The small boats anchored beside it bob about; one of them bears a name painted in black in large letters: *Jana*. Another is called: *Santa Cruz*.

Along the yellowish sandy shore, there are other boats; from here, they look as if they had been lined up in groups of two or three. Fishermen are dragging a net out of the water and leaving it spread out on the beach. A woman passes, carrying a load on her back, held in place by her *capulana*, while another, younger woman has a bundle of firewood on her head. Further on, beneath some thorn-trees, other women are selling fish.

Catembe is more relaxing than Costa do Sol, which is why it's better for talking and for flirtations, for letting things take their course, for the people who ought to get together to do so. Not that there aren't occasional surprises, pleasant and unpleasant: we can all see, for example, that Ditinha has her eye on Joaquim Barata, but it isn't clear whether he feels the same or prefers Titita. He seems to have his eye on both. And to be honest, we haven't yet worked out if Carolina really likes Tójó or if she's just pretending, so as to make it look as if she doesn't fancy Juvenal, when he, in fact, is the one she's after.

It took us all a long time to decipher Rodrigo as well, to find out whether or not he was interested in me. I said he wasn't, Ditinha disagreed, and Joana was a hundred per cent certain that he was. I would laugh and assure them that the only reason he looked at me was to annoy me, because that was what boys were like, they enjoyed needling us. A few years before, when their voices were just breaking and still occasionally emerged in fluting female tones, they used to sing: *Gita, Gita, estás tão bonita* – Gita, Gita, you're so pretty – and would wolf-whistle at me as I passed by trying to look entirely unamused, but laughing inside, because they were being both serious and not serious at all. I would pretend not to hear and avert my face, making my ponytail swing from side to side.

And the next day it would be Ditinha or Dita – *Dita, Dita, estás tão bonita* – and it would be her turn to get angry with them, and then we would both spin round and yell: 'Go on, whistle. See if we care.'

Rodrigo wasn't around then. Rodrigo was different, or so it seemed to us, because he hadn't always been part of the group. He had arrived from Beira at the end of the previous year and started going around with us because he had been put in the same class, but we didn't get the feeling that he really wanted to join in.

He usually turned up late, when the school bell was already ringing, and would enter the classroom almost at a run and sit down right at the back. He could be heard talking to the person next to him or tittering and making some ironic or mocking remark, then he would resume his distant air, which we found vaguely intriguing. Perhaps for us, or for me, he was something of an enigma. We didn't know what lay behind those pale eyes, the reluctant smile, the lips that quickly closed over his white teeth whenever he asked someone to lend him their notebook.

'Would you mind lending me your notes?' he asked me once, at the end of the first lesson, but just as I was about to answer, he grabbed my book and disappeared, giving me a wave of his hand as thanks. Then he'd follow me in the street, even though he would have had ample opportunity to talk to me earlier, if, at breaktime, he didn't join the group of boys who were always playing football, as if the mornings were one long game, which the lessons, unfortunately, kept interrupting.

He didn't even talk to me when he returned my notebook. When I went back to my place after the second break, I found the book on my desk with a note saying 'Thank you' scribbled on half a sheet of paper and pinned to the right-hand corner.

It seemed he had nothing to say to me, and yet he didn't take his eyes off me all morning. My desk was in the middle of the classroom, and every time I turned my head, I could see him looking at me. Needless to say, I found more reasons than usual to turn my head – to talk to Zaida or to Micas Julai, who both sat in the row behind, or to adjust my hairslide, pick up a pencil I had dropped on purpose or to see if the window at the back had been left open.

'It's windy,' Joana says in a complaining voice. 'Why did it have to be windy today of all days.'

'What do you mean "windy"?' says Alberta. 'There's no

151

wind at all, although there might be a heavy shower later. Look at that cloud.'

'If you talk about something bad, it will happen,' says Nuno. 'Don't tempt fate.'

'I saw a pangolin today,' says Juvenal in a quavering, mock-tearful voice. 'And that always brings bad luck.'

'Don't be so stupid!' we all say, laughing. And Tójó repeats this, drawing out the syllables: 'Stuuuupiiiid!'

We walk past some fishermen's houses made of wood and built on stilts because the land there used to flood. They're painted in various colours, mainly blue, white and rose pink, and the paint starts at ground level and mingles with the dust of the road. Some have a sort of porch or balcony because a part of the roof, also supported on stilts, sticks out. On the sand, and over the walls, nets have been hung out to dry in the sun.

An upturned rowing boat is lying next to another fitted with an outboard motor. The fishermen are sitting on the ground, mending nets, skilfully plying the shuttle. Beyond lies a scattering of banana and papaya trees and a line of straw huts made of wattle and daub and kambala wood. One hut has a notice fixed to it: The Open Window Shoeshop.

Further on, the waves beat against the sea wall – the Indian Ocean brown, earth-grey, and blue in the distance. An arrow tells us: Ponta do Ouro 117 km.

We walk along the sandy, dusty road, turning our backs on the houses on stilts.

Was it that day, or perhaps another, when it suddenly began to pour with rain and we had to run for shelter?

No, I think it was another day. We got separated as we ran, and at some point, I found myself with Roberto on one of the shanty-town roads, along which a few straw huts were built. A boy of about seven was standing at the door of one of these, staring out at us and the rain.

'Can we come in?' Roberto asked. The boy didn't answer, but moved aside to allow us to enter.

We went in, soaked to the skin, our hair dripping.

The rain was getting heavier and heavier, rattling on the roof like sieved sand. Great fat drops were coming in from above, where there was a gap just below the roof; it slid in shining threads down the wall where various items of clothing were hanging on nails, alongside cuttings from newspapers and magazines and a colour picture taken from a calendar.

'This is their bedroom,' I think as I sit on the floor (all three of us are sitting on a mat). In one corner is a sewing machine – it's incredible that a sewing machine can be squeezed into an area the size of a handkerchief divided in two by a piece of cloth hung over a length of string to act as a curtain. I know without even looking that on the other side is the kitchen: there'll be a table, a stove, buckets, plastic bowls and, hung from hooks on the wall, saucepans and frying pans.

The food though is cooked outside, on the fire lit beneath the three-legged cast-iron pots. I know, too, that outside there'll be the occasional green patch of sweet potato plants. And, unexpectedly, on either side of the doors there might be a raised and rather ramshackle flower bed, patiently constructed stone upon stone.

'What's your name?' asks Roberto.

'Henrique,' says the boy and smiles.

Perhaps there is a cloth or a sheet of plastic draped over the hut, secured by rocks at the corners. I didn't notice when we went in, but it seems possible given the amount of noise the rain is making. Hypnotised, we watch the rain beating down outside the door covered not by the usual red- or blue-painted piece of wood, but by a bead curtain made of seeds.

In one corner, on the floor, lies a lantern made from a flattened tin can with slits cut in the sides and a stump of candle in the middle. An oil lamp on top of a bench still smells of oil, but is probably empty.

Sometimes lamps like that fall over when lit while the people in the hut are sleeping, and the hut goes up in flames – the image is too horrible, and I close my eyes in order not to see it.

'We can go and find the others now,' says Roberto.

(The rain has stopped and the sun is suddenly shining again.)

'Thanks for letting us shelter in your house, Henrique,' we say, giving him a few coins as we leave.

I don't know if it was then that Roberto said, as we walked away:

'One day, the shanty town will swallow up the concrete city. That boy doesn't know it yet, but that's what he's waiting for.'

I don't know if he said that about Henrique or about some other child. Perhaps it was on another occasion. Roberto had been my best friend for a long time, and we had been insepar-able since junior school. We used to talk endlessly and agreed on almost everything. When I think about those days, he's the person I see, alongside Rodrigo. They were both, each in his own way, the centre of that world.

Roberto has a girlfriend. A *xiluva*, a flower, whom I've never seen and whose name I don't even know because she's not at school with us and didn't finish junior school. But she is all he thinks of and talks about and she's the one he's going to marry when the time is right. A lovely girl, a poppet, a flower, he says.

Sometimes I think that the only reason I don't fall in love with Roberto, and he with me, has less to do with Rodrigo and more to do with that girl, who fills his world.

True, Rodrigo's eyes drive me wild, and Roberto's eyes, shining out of his black face from behind his thick-lensed glasses, seem colder and more distant, but more intelligent too, and that only makes them all the more seductive.

Rodrigo's eyes are blue. Or are they green? I'm never sure because they change with the light. And it's perhaps that uncertainty that makes me look at them so much – I find them disquieting, intriguing, because they're never the same. I always feel a need to take a second look to make sure I wasn't wrong and that they really are blue. Or that I was wrong after all because they're actually green. And I always feel unsure – can you trust someone if you never know what colour his eyes are?

To us at the time, mathematics and philosophy had about all the allure of dead languages.

The school consisted of a ground floor and two other floors, and there were plenty of windows everywhere; the various buildings were connected by a series of galleries open on both sides, but with a roof to shelter us from the sun and the rain. Beyond the gates, in the area of reddish earth outside, bushes and shrubs had been planted as well as four large trees, one in each corner. By the time we reached the main door, having crossed that space, our sandals – or, if it was winter, our shoes – were covered in dust.

That year, we had our classes on the top floor, from which we would race downstairs when the final bell rang at the end of school. (The rush, the voices, the shouts, the laughter, the scamper down the stairs in which the facing wall was made of large expanses of glass from landing to landing, right down to the bottom.)

In the last class, though, the time really dragged. I would glance at my watch and then look again, surreptitiously holding it to my ear to check that it was working, then gaze in despair at the window. Outside lay the street, flowers peeping over the walls, green acacias. From where I was sitting all I could see was a scrap of sky, not even very blue, our sky being so unstable and so readily filled with clouds.

Rosário is only twenty-two, not much older than me.

'Have you got a boyfriend?' I ask her, and she roars with laughter: 'Yáyáyáyáyá'.

She's willing to talk about her sister though: 'He gave our family bride gifts.' And shortly afterwards, she announces: 'She going to have a baby.' And she bursts out laughing again.

It's always the same, she laughs at everything and nothing and responds to almost every question with: 'Yáyáyáyáyá', which is her very jolly way of saying 'Yes'. Sometimes she sounds just like a *xirico* bird.

At other times, I find that foolish laugh irritating, bubbling up as it does, whatever the reason, sensible or non-sensical — a laugh that begins as a titter and ends as a guffaw. And she sways her hips when she laughs as if she were making fun of us.

And yet that is precisely why Laureano likes her, because there is such a lack of laughter in our house. As for working, the clothes are never washed, the house is never cleaned, the supper never cooked. And when you run your finger over the table, it makes a line in the dust. 'Haven't you ever worked before?' I asked her a few months ago.

She replied: 'Yáyáyáyáyá,' but showed no desire to learn how to do anything.

'You're a complete disaster,' I sigh, and she explodes into giggles again, as if I had paid her a compliment.

'We could at least get a cook,' I say to Laureano. 'Like everyone else.'

He agrees, but does nothing about it. And so I stop worrying as well. Too bad if the house is dirty and untidy, Rosário will do as she pleases. As for me, I have other things to think about.

Although, to be honest, she does annoy me a great deal, for example, with the way she stands at the window to see who's passing, meanwhile leaving me to do the housework. And then there's the radio, which she has on all day, very loud, in the kitchen. When I ask her to turn it down, she says, as she always does, 'Yáyáyáyáyá', and a minute later the radio is blasting out again, just as if I didn't exist. And at other times, she goes all sulky and sullen, as if any work she did for us were an enormous favour.

The road that leads to the school is lined with trees. I travel in the bus, almost from one side of the city to the other, but now, after classes, I prefer to walk a couple of stops, just for the pleasure of strolling along the wide pavement under the trees. And what do I look at? Houses, roofs, windows, flowers peeping over walls, the broad leaves of banana trees slowly swaying – there's almost always at least one that's untouched and complete, while the others have been torn and tattered by the wind.

I walk for the pure pleasure of walking – and because someone is following me. Even without looking round, I can hear the footsteps behind me, and yet they never grow faster, rather, they stop sometimes or slacken their pace, as if they didn't want to catch me up, as if, perhaps, they would betray themselves if they ever came too close and became visible.

Nevertheless, he's definitely following me. Rodrigo, that is. Protected by that short distance of two or three steps. Perhaps waiting for a gesture from me, waiting for me to give him a signal, to show that I've noticed his presence by turning round. But I won't do that because I'm afraid he might laugh at me, and so I walk on beneath the trees, watching the spots of sunlight on the pavement and sniffing the wind like an animal let loose in a field, glad to be alive and moving its body in the sun and the light and breathing in the smell of summer.

And yet it could be so simple: he could walk up to me, say 'Hello' and then whatever else came into his head. And I, too, could smile and say 'Hello' and whatever else came into my head.

Or he could join me now, under the mahogany trees, in the little square outside the school, where there's a round stone fountain in the middle of the red earth. He could sit beside me on the steps that lead to the road that goes down to the coast.

But perhaps it's not easy for boys either, perhaps they feel equally insecure, I think, when I look at them, trying to understand why they're always fighting and arguing and why they seem to have a constant need to challenge each other, Roberto and João Saiote, Tójó, Joaquim, Juvenal, Ibrahim and Ramesh. They laugh loudly because they're afraid, they hide their feelings as if such things were embarrassing, they mask their shyness with arrogance.

They, too, are preparing themselves, as are we. Childhood is over, they say to the Black boy when he is circumcised, while he weeps with pain. He is given another name and cannot look back, as the flames grow higher and burn down the encampment where he died in order to be born again. And when he returns to the village, his mother uncovers his feet, first the right and then the left, to show that he can now walk through life as an adult. He couldn't do so before because a child's feet cannot go very far, they're trammelled, tangled in the scrub, pierced by thorns.

And when Black girls have their first period, they are anointed with plant oils, adorned with necklaces, earrings and bracelets, and their hair is arranged in a different way.

Yesterday, child, you did not exist, you were just a small living creature, they say, as they sing and dance. Yesterday, you did not exist, you were not a person, yesterday, you were a stone. Now you are a woman, you have found your place among the people. And the village chief sprinkles flour on the girl's bowed head and she takes a different name because she has died and been born again. And she might be called 'Green Branch', 'Desired One', 'You're not

Alone', or 'Attractive in Love' because now she is different. She is the initiate who has solved enigmas and can decipher dreams.

Ancient customs, still maintained by some, I read in a book.

It occurs to me, though, that the only true initiation is our first encounter with the opposite sex, because only then do we know our own.

As I walk down the street, I think: the body is the site of that knowledge, the only knowledge that counts.

It's the season for the dances that begin the rituals, the rites of passage, says Roberto. And then I notice, for the first time that night, the music of an ancient, almost decrepit band that has been playing for several hours on the bandstand – old, distant songs that get lost in our ears and can be heard only in sudden brief bursts. (It's a night of celebration and we're strolling beneath the trees in the park.)

I thought about Rodrigo, and thinking about him was like repeating his name (Rodriiiiiiiiigooooo!). I was calling him even though he couldn't hear and even as I was about to fall asleep, I would desperately repeat his name.

And one day, as if in answer to that call, he somehow drew near, and I suddenly realised that he had leapt the gap separating us and had been walking beside me for some time, indeed, we had walked almost the whole length of the street, beneath the acacias.

'To the sea,' he says softly, almost as if it were a question.

I nod, clutching my notebooks, my heart pounding.

'To the sea,' I repeat, as if those words translated an obvious fact, or as if in some way it calmed me to know that we had some apparent objective.

But he's looking at me, and I'm looking at him and at his oblique gaze that slides over my shoulders, down to my waist and plunges down below the round neckline of my dress.

I don't know what else we talk about, perhaps nothing. We have gone round the corner and are following another street, and as we progress, I feel I'm losing solidity and strength. I'm glad when a bus stops and we get on it – afterwards, I realise that I didn't even notice where it was going. We're sitting side by side on a seat and watching through the windows as the acacias are left behind.

We finally get off, it's hot, but there's a breeze, we cross noisy streets where the doors stand half-open, affording us a glimpse into dark houses from which come the shouts of children and scolding voices, we pass shops displaying their merchandise, chinaware, rugs, postcards, wicker chairs and piles of bags, then the people disappear and there are shattered doors, abandoned gardens that have become dumping grounds for junk, boxes, broken furniture, scrap metal, we pass the warehouse area, the cranes and hoists, the wagons, the boats along the quay.

Before us are the moored ships, whose dark green hulls reveal rust-eaten anchors. And when we finally stop walking and he starts to kiss me, I feel that I have lost all powers of resistance: he doesn't need to use persuasion, it would take only a breeze to pin me against the wall. It's his desire for me that makes him so rough, I think, and I feel almost proud of the urgency with which he presses his mouth to mine, the haste with which his hand fumbles for the top button of my blouse, almost wrenching it off, proud of his hardening body pushing between my thighs despite my skirt. My skirt, I feel, should not exist, but I won't help him undo the other buttons on my blouse because my arms have closed about his body and my hands are clutching his head, the back of his neck. (Now, I feel, nothing else exists.)

Finding a place where we could be alone became an idée fixe with us and, over time, almost an obsession. Naked and alone, with no one else around. A 'place' for us alone, not a public place or a common place.

No, café terraces and cinemas were not enough for us then, even though we almost always went to the Sunday matinees. I remember what the Scala looked like inside: we enter the foyer with its red walls and white marble floor edged in black, an edging which, on the stairs leading to the balcony, becomes a broad band up the middle. We don't take the stairs, we buy stalls seats and advance patiently, hand in hand, caught up in the queue of people who sometimes push against us, almost forcing us apart. At last, we sit down in the back row of the blue-velvet-upholstered seats, facing the stage where a gilt frame surrounds the screen.

'It's sort of art nouveau all this,' says Rodrigo, pointing to the white glass neon lamps in the form of a folded sheet of paper, the large rectangles with geometric patterns, the walls painted light blue.

But we're not looking at the lamps because we like the style, all we want is for the lights to go down so that we can feel that we're alone, hand in hand, and only occasionally watching the film, which doesn't really interest us, kissing in the dark with the feeling that we're not being observed, because we're in the back row and there's no one sitting behind us. (His hand on my knees, on the light fabric of my dress. His hand slipping between my knees, lifting the light fabric of my dress.)

This was also a time of talking and shared confidences. A time to find out that his mother died several years ago, to see a photo of her sitting in the garden, her hands folded on her floral skirt, a straw hat shading her face. Still young and pretty in the photograph. Not yet dead.

A time to learn that his father would shout: 'Now you listen to me!'

He spoke each word as if he had picked up a chisel and were hammering it into his wife's head, and she would cover her ears and shout even louder so as not to hear. And his father would stamp his feet and keep hammering those words into her ears, harder and harder, as if he wanted to burst her eardrums.

Each word was a stone. And his wife's head would begin to bleed, above her eyebrows and in the middle of her forehead. The blood dribbled from her ears.

I don't know if that's quite how he described it, but that was how I imagined his parents duelling over the supper table: his father throws a knife at his wife's mouth and cuts her lip, which begins to bleed, then he throws another sharper knife at her shoulder and a fork at each eye, but this time he misses. And his mother hurls a plate at the wall, and both parents fling glasses at each other's head, water glasses, wine glasses, liqueur glasses. Rodrigo is still very young and tries not to pay any attention because it happens every mealtime. When his mother cries too loudly, his father turns up the volume on the radio so that the neighbours won't hear. And the next meal will be the same.

He told me this, even though he might not have used those words. And I told him how Amélia had left three years before. Even though it was hard for me to talk about it, because I no longer had a clear image of her. She was a body in flight, for whom there was no turning back.

She took almost nothing, apart from a few clothes, I tell him. I was the one who emptied the wardrobes and the drawers, at first stuffing it all into bags, without picking and choosing or even looking. Later, I sorted through it, read letters and papers, found photographs. I think she left those things for me, like pieces in a jigsaw puzzle, so that one day I would be able to recreate her image.

She kept newspaper cuttings and horoscopes, underlined beauty advice in articles signed by Alegna d'Ortsac, I told him.

Some she had torn up, but she kept the torn scraps, on which she had written in red pencil: Alegna is a lie. And the letters she had written to Bob Pereira had obviously been signed Patrícia Hart because that was the name on the envelopes containing the letters he sent to her. Bob Pereira — yes, in answer to an advertisement. Just as she had done once before, with Laureano. Perhaps, that was it: yes, in a way, she was repeating the same story.

When I think of her, I imagine her walking round and round in circles as if she were bewitched. Amélia, who was so afraid of spells.

Bob Pereira. The name is ridiculous. As is his photo. She left a photograph of him as well: a fat man wearing a felt hat, standing beside a blue convertible, in front of a prefabricated wooden house. I know the car is blue because it's a colour photo.

But I don't want to talk about that now. I put everything back in a bag and stow it behind the empty suitcases at the very top of a wardrobe. One day, I'll take a closer look. But not now. Now, put your arms around me.

Yes, Laureano tried to stop her. He tried to close the door, but she was standing at the top of the stairs screaming that she was leaving.

The conversation they had on the verandah. As interminable as those they used to have in the sewing-room. Darkness falling. Silence all around. The noises of the night that somehow didn't disturb the silence — the frogs' croaking, the soft flight of bats, the moths hurling themselves against the mosquito nets at the windows. In the dark, you could hear the muffled thud and flutter of their wings.

Perhaps there was nothing more to be said. And then she left.

I believe she and Bob Pereira exchanged letters, and then, one day, he came to fetch her. She left with him on the same boat. As if it were an easy thing to do: quickly pack your suitcase and leave, taking with you the bare minimum, almost, you might say, leaving nothing behind.

Laureano – I prefer to talk to you about him as he was when I was a child. Doing repairs, happy and whistling softly to himself, thinking his own thoughts. He put things back on track. Whatever disaster might befall the house, he was there – the walls could fall in, the windows shatter, and he would restore everything to its proper place. He would arrive at the end of the day with paint and brushes, varnish and glue and that knack of his for putting the pieces together again. He ruled over the world of objects: the tap in the wash-tub, the wastepipe in the bath, the gas pipes, the gas ring, the wall socket, all the things that were beyond us, beyond Amélia and me and even Lóia, and that would leave us feeling alone and frightened. He was undaunted; he took those things on and won. The house was clean and tidy and in working order. The Black House, the one that danced in the wind.

Now, though, he sits in his aviator's chair, eyes closed, the cat asleep on his lap. His hair is white, he has lines around his eyes and mouth and wears old-fashioned glasses.

A bird that fell to earth, I think, a bird that didn't open its wings in time and could never fly again.

He was the one who first told me about them, a long time ago, about the yellow birds that live in the jungle around the Zambezi, birds that feed on ripe fruit, scoop up water as they skim the surface of rivers and lakes, and drop from the trees with their wings furled, only opening them once they're air-borne. They have to be careful, of course, because if they don't open their wings in time, they crash to the ground and can never lift off again. Then, all you have to do is reach out your hand and pick them up.

He liked to tell me these things. Perhaps because he'd had so little schooling himself, which he always considered a great misfortune (although it's taken me a long time to understand why), he gave great importance to those scraps of knowledge, to the apparently unimportant details that he stored away in his memory, like precious things – the names of trees and insects and the tributaries of rivers. Or perhaps it was simply the way he was, attentive, alert, looking at things with a degree of attention that was also a form of love.

When I was a child, he showed me how the fully-grown thorn tree has thorns as small as those on a rosebush, whereas when it's only a bush, it's covered in huge, white thorns, about a span long, which later drop off. He showed me how the leaves of the mango tree were longer and thinner than those of the cashew tree, and pointed out the unmistakable papaya tree, with its cluster of fruits round the top of the trunk and its branches on which the leaves all seemed to grow out of the same point. Small everyday miracles that your eye could always alight on as if for the first time.

But when he sits in his aviator's chair now and looks around, he sees nothing. His greying head droops onto his chest, the newspaper, forgotten, falls to the floor. His hand reaches blindly for the glass of beer. He was never the same after Amélia left. She took all his joy with her.

He used to forget to change his sweaty shirt. I had to hide it, stick it in the wash-tub, scrub it thoroughly with soap and water, then leave him a nice clean shirt where he could see it on the bedstead. His gestures were those of an automaton, a sleep-walker, as if he wasn't quite awake. He was distracted and often didn't hear what you said, sometimes looking up and saying: 'Hm?', as if he had come from far away or wasn't even there.

He ate little, less and less each day, as if he found it hard to eat. He would chew away at small mouthfuls of food and then stretch his neck forward in order to swallow. Most of the food remained on his plate and had to be thrown away.

The nights were particularly difficult. Like when someone dies. I would wake up sometimes with the birds and the other dawn sounds – doors opening, water gurgling and hissing like a snake through the house's ancient plumbing. I would hear him go out into the street and I didn't know if he had simply got up very early or never been to bed. Sometimes he would leave the radio on all day and possibly all night – the voices of the presenters, a man and a woman, and then music. At night, the music was quieter and the voices took on an intimate tone, as if they really were company. But it was hard to get through the night. Just like when someone dies.

And there was the way he came down the stairs, clinging to the banister. You would think he would fall if he didn't have some support or would be lost if he didn't have something to hold on to at all times. Even the smallest gesture seemed an enormous effort.

His rifle grew dusty, he never again went partridge-shooting with Agripino, Relito and Jamal; Licínio had to suffer his bouts of 'phylloxera' alone; the yard filled up with weeds and the castor-oil tree withered and died.

Later, he entered a phase of frenetic activity, as if he couldn't bear his hands to be idle. He put new wire around the chicken run, caught a cicada and built a cage for it, dug and re-dug the flower beds. All of this without saying a word, because he had virtually stopped talking, except for the occasions when I found him speaking to Simba the cat.

I talked about Lóia too, I'm sure I did. Oddly enough, though, it's not Rodrigo I remember talking to about her, but Roberto.

Lóia was connected to the everyday world of the Blacks, to the poor areas that surrounded us – low houses, painted and made of odd bits of random material, and that looked like children's drawings or abandoned stage-sets, fading in the sun: a door, two windows, one on each side, and below them a band of colour in bright blue, yellow or pink. Above, a thin, rickety roof, occasionally also daubed with paint. And at the front door there was generally a step or two, to bridge the gap between house and street.

You could see into the houses through the open doors: disconnected bits and pieces, a table, a bed in the middle of a room, a broken wardrobe, a disembowelled armchair, and somewhere you could hear a radio playing loudly, the sound of voices, a child crying or a woman.

Outside, there would be old people sitting, children playing in the gutter, a mangy dog lying in the shade.

One day, Lóia didn't come back. One day and another and another. I wanted to go with Laureano to the *caniço* to find her, and sometimes on a Sunday afternoon, reluctantly and with a heavy heart, he would take me there and we would wander aimlessly around.

The wind whips up the dust, lizards scurry over the uneven ground, then stop, pretending to be dead, petrified with fear, before scurrying madly off again. A man passes, toothpick in mouth, another is cleaning his teeth with a *mulala* stick. Clothes are draped over a window ledge, beside a bird that hops about inside its cage. Girls in grubby dresses are walking about barefoot, hand in hand. A look of amazement in their huge eyes. Another is carrying a sleeping baby over whose mouth flies are crawling. The desolate streets of the Black people. As if nothing mattered and everything that was going wrong would, inevitably, only get worse. Dead people walking about in the light of day.

In the end, Laureano doesn't know what further excuses to give and tells me, hesitantly, as if the words weighed on him: 'Lóia – has gone to live far away. Zedequias got a new job, and they all went with him.'

'But where?' I ask, startled, hanging on his words, not sure yet whether to believe him or not.

'To – Mocímboa da Praia,' I hear him say.

But that was in another place and on another day. Not yet. Now there's only the fixed sun and the emptiness all around. As if everyone were dead.

Yes, it was all a nightmare – or a dream. The lizard again

careering madly through the dust, propelling itself forward with rapid movements of its tail, the stray cat watching from a windowsill, motionless silhouettes in doorways, sitting on mats or on the sandy floor. Even the loud radio didn't seem to break the silence, as if no one were listening.

Meanwhile, the rainy season arrived and, as usual, the city was divided in two, which was a blessing on one side and a curse on the other: in the city of the Whites, the rain washed the buildings and the streets clean, watered the gardens and caused flowers to bloom, but it opened deep wounds in the city of the Blacks, which was transformed into a swamp. The sand became mud, the ditches overflowed with excrement; filthy, stinking water and detritus invaded the houses.

Between the concrete city and the airport, the swamp filled everything and was everything – filth, flies, piles of rubbish, sewers, putrid smells, parasites, and mosquitos that would spread still further when the wind was in the wrong direction.

'They can cause fatal diseases,' Laureano says, 'or diseases that stay with you for ever, because they mark you for life.' (I remember Amélia and her fear of the swamp. Perhaps she had been right.)

The government (I know that some grave, negative remark will follow whenever he begins a sentence with that word) doesn't just *allow* building in that area, it actually ordered houses to be built there. That's all it has to offer the Blacks.

Children play in the mud. Further on, kneeling on the ground, a woman is struggling to light a fire that refuses to light.

That is when he suddenly stops and says that Lóia, Zedequias and the children have moved far away.

A fire that won't light, a fire that won't light. A woman struggling to light a fire. Kneeling on the ground.

So that's what happened, I think, bursting into tears. She went to Mocímboa da Praia and never came back.

In a way, though, the news is a relief. When I think of Lóia she's not in that desert of dirt and mud, but in a different place that I can imagine: there are green waves and a long tongue of sand, with fishing nets spread out in the sun. And beside it, there's a river, just like in Macaneta.

Zedequias is now a fisherman, and the boat he sails in is long and narrow, like an *almadia*, a kind of bark canoe. He returns in the evening with the fish he has caught, and Orquídea and Ló are running around on the sand.

Lóia was far away, but I accepted that loss. She hadn't dissolved into air or been transformed into a bird or sand or a leaf. She existed somewhere. Mocímboa da Praia was a real place, and that was reassuring. I found it on the map, in the north of the country. There would be long lines of coconut palms. The wind would set the leaves flapping.

(The wind, like someone's breath, blowing over the mat. The great African night all around, the silence full of noises. The shrill cries of crickets, the rustle of mice, the blind flight of bats – their short, wheeling flights, suddenly swooping down low by the door, as if performing somersaults in the dark. Devil-spirits whistling in the trees. Devil-bats playing. The open fire on cold June and July nights. The summer rain falling on the scrub. Children crying in their sleep.

Picking mushrooms in the forest after the rains. The fire kept alight to fend off animals because in the night there is always the eye of some creature watching – utterly still and bright – when you go further into the jungle, where you have to make sure you have a fetish with you so that you don't meet an enemy animal when you go for water, carrying a can on your head. Animals slip into our dreams and children turn over on their mats as they sleep.)

Only years later did he tell me that Lóia had died in hospital of tuberculosis. Zedequias came to tell him that she was ill and coughing up blood. Laureano took her to the Miguel Bombarda Hospital, and visited her until the end.

We went together to the cemetery and saw the gravestone he had ordered to be placed there: Lourdes Panquene. And two dates. The first was merely an approximate number, which he had calculated by counting backwards from Orquídea's birth. Lóia never knew exactly which year she had been born in, nor did Zedequias, but that was fairly common at the time. Strict records weren't kept, and in the villages in the interior, time was measured differently. They would say, for example, many harvests ago, in the year of the great rains or in the year of the locusts.

So there were the name and the two dates. Not even that really: Lourdes Panquene just didn't sound like her.

Later, Laureano told me why he had chosen the town of Mocímboa da Praia when he lied to me: it was the first name that came into his head, perhaps because he'd heard it so often over the loudspeakers at the airport, a voice calling passengers for flights going to Beira, Nampula, Porto Amélia and Mocímboa da Praia.

'Laureano should get married again,' I say to Rodrigo. 'To some sweet woman who would make him happy. I could live with them, but I'd rather live with you. A small one-bedroom apartment would be enough.'

We laugh and hold hands under the table. It seems so simple. And so difficult. I don't have the money to rent my own apartment, nor does Laureano. And Rodrigo's father, given what I've heard about him, certainly wouldn't contribute anything, and so Rodrigo has no money either, apart from the small monthly allowance he gets. If we add it all up, how much does it come to? We do our sums and shake our heads.

'Unless the woman had a job too,' I say. Yes, a woman who liked Laureano just as he was. And had some money of her own, an income. A woman who would wait for him at the end of the day with a smile on her lips and supper ready on the table. And one who wouldn't mind helping out Rodrigo and me.

But where to find such a woman? I don't know anyone remotely like that. Besides, it's not up to me to find her. He's free to live his own life, as am I.

'He's always left me free to do as I want,' I say. 'And that's the thing I'm most grateful to him for really.'

It was around then that Joana went on holiday to Portugal with her family and when she returned, she had a lot to tell.

Living there was just awful, she said, everything was forbidden. Even going out with someone. You couldn't go to the cinema with a boy because it might 'look bad', in fact, they lived in terror of 'looking bad'. You couldn't even breathe for fear it might look bad. For example, one day, her Aunt Delfina was walking along the street with her umbrella open to keep off the wind, and her sister, Aunt Celestina, suddenly nudged her hard in the ribs and said: 'Close your umbrella, will you. It's not raining and everyone's staring at us.' And when Aunt Delfina took no notice, she started in on her again: 'What will people say, we look like real fools walking along with an umbrella up when it's not even raining.'

You're joking, we all said, laughing, but Joana went on:

And the girls wouldn't ever dream of wearing trousers, because that's what boys wear and, of course, it would 'look bad', and obviously they'd never wear shorts, and if you wore a bikini it would be the end of the world; there was a special inspector on the beaches who went round checking to see that women's bathing suits were decent.

You're joking, we said, roaring with laughter. It just wasn't possible, she was obviously making it all up.

But Joana assured us that it really was like that, all very composed and orderly. The girls resembled prim little saints and walked around as if they were permanently on their way to a party, because they had to catch a boy's eye from a distance, given that no boy could actually approach them – because everything 'looked bad'. It looked bad to sit down with boys on the seafront, and going out alone at night was even worse, which is why they almost always had someone else sitting close by when they were talking to a boy, so that it wouldn't look bad.

And they were afraid of everything, they wouldn't take a step without glancing to either side, in case they were either getting ahead of the others or slipping behind; the streets were very narrow, and everything was small and mean, people clung together like a bunch of grapes, parents grand-parents cousins godparents colleagues godchildren neigh-bours, all of them done up to the nines and unable to breathe for lack of air.

And they gossiped constantly of course, they would say, for example: 'I saw your daughter today', which wasn't a way of showing attention or interest, but of tightening the net and exercising control. They knew where everyone was at any moment because someone was always watching, plus there weren't that many places to go, there was one street or, at most, two streets with shops in them and that was that, you went there to see and be seen, but girls weren't allowed to walk up and down the street more than twice on the same morning or afternoon, they could walk once up one side and once down the other and then they had to go straight home, otherwise they might give the impression that they were on the hunt for a boyfriend and that, naturally, could look bad.

Nicely-brought-up young ladies spent the afternoons at the hairdressers, staring out of the window as they awaited their turn, because having your hair done took hours; they would wait in line there, and spend from lunch until supper sitting on little stools chewing their fingernails and leafing through magazines, and the hairdressers always spoke to them in an affected, over-familiar voice, as if they were related: have you seen this, did you know that.

And you had to keep alert in the street to make sure that you spotted anyone you knew because if you inadvertently walked past some acquaintance or didn't greet him or her effusively enough, they might cold-shoulder you or turn against you.

No one ever talked about politics because it was too dangerous and that's why the newspapers, friends, relatives and neighbours all said the same thing, namely, nothing.

What a narrow, torpid life, I think, as I look at the photos of my cousins Marivone and Delmira, dressed for their first communion or for Carnival. Their faces look drab and almost stupid. They attend a girls-only school and never go out with boys and if they ever do go to a dance, once a year at most, an aunt sits at the table and watches them all night to see if their partner gets too close or squeezes them too tight. And since they can only dance with boys they know, the aunt immediately makes a note of the partner's name because she probably wants to find out everything, not just about the boy, but about his family too. My cousins cripple their feet by wearing shoes that are far too small for them because they're scared to death that their perfectly normal-sized feet will look inelegant; they straighten the organdi bows at the waist of their dress and, despite all the advice they've received, immediately miss the beat.

They have to be virgins when they go to the altar because, if not, the country would collapse and the world come to an end. And at school they all line up to sing patriotic songs like 'Flowering tree reach out your branches to the passing youth'.

It's so obvious, I think, I can see it so clearly, all it takes is a quick glance at a photo.

Rosário is standing at the gate, talking to the postman. They're both roaring with laughter – I've already noticed how she's always watching from the windows and makes a special effort to look smart whenever it's time for the milkman, postman or fishmonger to call.

I smile at the haste with which she says goodbye to the postman as soon as she sees me coming down the street, and she rapidly closes the door as if caught out doing something she shouldn't.

'You can flirt with whoever you like, I don't care,' I say as I go into the house and laugh in her frowning face.

Narciso writes now and then, always telling us how well life is treating him: in one letter he'd just bought a house in a cooperative housing scheme, in another he was about to go off on holiday to Spain, and in yet another he had just made the tenth payment on his car.

Narciso, whose education was paid for by his mother from the money Laureano sent her. He's an engineer now and he writes to show how much better his life is than his brother's.

'That's the only reason he writes,' I tell Roberto, 'to humiliate him. Otherwise, he has no interest in us at all, and never a word of gratitude or affection.'

People, I realise, like to lord it over others.

This was evident even at Sunday mass, especially at the Cathedral or the church of Santo António da Polana: those with the means and the power went there in order to be seen and to meet and greet others as they left after the service, and while you were expected to wear expensive clothes, you were also expected to go for an unaffected, almost sporty look, and if the whole thing hadn't been so utterly hypocritical, it would have made a rather nice show, the family lined up in the pew, the father still youthful despite his grey hair, the mother preferably a few years younger, but always elegantly dressed, and beside them, their children, equally well-groomed and smart. Splendid cars wait outside, where Black chauffeurs with gleaming buttons on their uniforms are busily opening and closing doors.

This was what mattered to them, this, for them, was the real mass, however contrite, absorbed and almost humble they might look when it came to making confession or taking communion. It was all humbug and pretence. They went there to affirm not their equality with others, but their privileged position, and they left the service determined to continue to live in exactly the same way. Why change when everything was already so well ordered, with them ruling and others serving, now and for ever, Amen.

Meanwhile, the priest turned to the congregation and, opening wide his arms, said: 'Dear brothers and sisters.'

But it wasn't true, and the priests could see that it was all hypocrisy, although they pretended not to.

Because afterwards, says Roberto, they sit down with their silver cutlery to eat their Sunday prawn or lobster curry served by Black servants wearing white gloves, while the Blacks in their straw huts eat locust curry and fat rats roasted on a spit, and the mice nibble at their sleeping children.

And yet no one and no culture is better than any other, and the Whites have a lot to learn from the Blacks, I say. For example, the Blacks never hit their children, they talk to them and discuss the events of the day, and that way the children learn that there's a time to work and a time to rest, a time to dance and a time to sleep, that there's a place for life and a place for death, for joy and sadness, a place for human beings and for what is above and beyond us.

A part of what we harvest is offered to the spirits because we are not the masters of the natural world, merely its inhabitants. We offer seeds or flour to show that we know our limits and know that Nature is larger than us. And so a part always returns to her, and we dare not touch it.

That, among other things, is what I learned from Africa: the smallness of we human beings compared to the vastness of all that is not human. We are nothing, mere dust in the wind, tiny figures in an immense landscape.

We need very little really because we ourselves are little: we need to satisfy our thirst, our hunger and our sexual desire, to have a mat to sleep on and to be at peace with our heart.

Laureano always lived like that, and I can understand why. It's an age-old wisdom.

I also learned from Africa that real life is slow. Only the dead are in a frantic hurry. And the foolish.

But there are also things that need to be changed in Africa, says Roberto. The enmities among Blacks themselves, for example, or the way women are treated: the woman carries the children, the water and the wood, and the man walks beside her like a king, while she carries everything, like a donkey pulling a cart. The women work from dawn to dusk and often get beaten for their pains; sometimes they enter into a loveless marriage simply because it suits the family; and the best food is always kept for the husband; when he sits down at the table, she doesn't sit down with him, she eats the leftovers; and in some situations, it's her mother-in-law who rules the roost and beats her too. That's why sometimes women run away, go down to the river in search of crocodiles, hang themselves from trees or flee into the jungle until they drop from hunger, thirst or exhaustion.

Or else they're abandoned, along with their children, because their man has gone north or south in search of a better life, although that can also be an excuse, when the man in question is as irresponsible as a child and wants to return to his bachelor existence.

Or else one man has several wives who have to get along

with each other, even if they're horribly jealous of the wife he favours most or the one who has just had a child.

The ability to survive passes through them, I say. They're bound to the earth, to cultivating the fields, to the old customs, to their children, there is a long line of time that passes through them and of which they are the guardians, unaware of the importance of everything under their guardianship – the gestures of rocking a child to sleep, of sowing, harvesting, lighting a fire, grinding maize.

When the men lose their way, they always go back to the women, says Roberto. When they get too carried away by having cars and money, by White ideas that they'd like to put into practice but without success, when they don a cap and a uniform and think they're a cut above their neighbour because of the shiny buttons on their jacket – then it's the women they turn to because women don't lose their way and can tell the difference between real gold and false.

(His *xiluva*, I think, his flower. His *xiluva* sweetheart.)

There are so many things in the world that need changing, we sigh. But changing the world doesn't seem so very difficult to us. All it takes is a few like-minded people working together for things to begin to change.

Then, suddenly, war broke out. Like a minefield exploding. It was no surprise to anyone, we knew it would happen, it had in other places, and sooner or later, it was bound to reach us.

Portugal was an ill-governed place. Badly run. Lisbon refuses to talk to the Africans. He had always said that. And now here it was. Said Laureano.

We were saddened to think of those who would die. On both sides. But were there really two sides? The men crossing the sea from Lisbon didn't want that absurd war either.

Only a little longer, we said. Only a little longer and the social order in Portugal will collapse too, like a fragile house of cards.

When I was a child, the Old Man – Salazar – looked to me just like my grandfather, I tell Roberto. My grandfather fell off the roof and died when he was chasing Laureano with his stick and his belt.

Dictators always fall in the end, I say, because that story, in my version of events, seems to me symbolic. From a roof, a window, a chair or a bench – they always fall in the end from something that might not even be that high, that might even be on the ground itself. Because, without them realising it, we have been tunnelling under them all this time until, at last, they begin to sink. We have been digging tunnels underneath them like ants, like moles, and suddenly they fall, because their support has gone. The very ground on which they were sitting just opens up beneath them.

It was then that we had the idea of making a poster. A large piece of paper on which we would write in giant letters that could be seen from a distance: 'Independence for Mozambique'. Then we would unfurl it in the middle of the room at the dance held for the final-year students.

We would secretly pin it up on the wall underneath another poster advertising the band, although it wasn't yet clear who it would be, whether I Cinque di Roma or Shegundo Galarza. At the height of the party, when everyone was on the dance floor, we would remove the first poster with a flourish, revealing the one we had made underneath, with the message clear for all to see.

We thought it was a wonderful idea, and just thinking about it gave us a real thrill. Tomorrow, we decided, we'll go and buy the paint.

When she sees me, Orquídea waves gaily from the other end of the corridor and, with mop and bucket in hand, walks towards me over the floor she has just cleaned and which is still damp and shining.

'Gitita!' she calls, oblivious to the other people hurrying past at visiting time. A nurse closes the door to one of the rooms, places a stern finger on her lips and says: 'Sh!'

Orquídea ignores her and the passers-by, throws down both bucket and mop and says loudly over and over as she embraces me: 'Gitita!'

She readjusts her headscarf − which slipped off as we embraced − leans on a window ledge and tells me the latest news: she's got a different boyfriend, and one of her neighbours has had another baby, just a week ago. The change of boyfriend is a good thing because the one she had before was always going out with other women and made Orquídea cry a lot. Anyway, in the end, she got fed up with it. And she tells me his name, of the new boyfriend, that is − Aldemiro Cabanal − not the old one, Alfredo, who used to flirt with all the girls, his hat at a rakish angle and a toothpick in the corner of his mouth, and who would watch her crying and not say a word, not even bothering to spit out his toothpick.

Ló is still missing a lot of school, she says with a sigh. Fanisse wants her at home, to look after the smaller children. (There were two other children − Zedequias had another wife and other children, apart from Lóia, and after she died, he married yet another younger one, Fanisse. Ló likes her, but Orquídea doesn't and they often quarrel.)

'And what about you, Gitita, what about you?'

I, in turn, tell her what's been happening in my life. I usually go to see Orquídea when I'm at one of two emotional extremes, either when everything's going so well that I just have to tell her about it or when everything's going so badly that I can't keep it to myself any longer.

Once a month, since Amélia's departure, she and Ló come and have Sunday lunch with us.

'Let me borrow this one,' she says, opening my wardrobe and trying on skirts and dresses in the mirror.

By the following month, the fabric has faded, the skirt is torn and the zip has broken, because, in the meantime, she has been blithely lending it out to all her girlfriends, and she won't agree not to. That's the custom and that's how they live; things circulate: clothes, fridges, saucepans are never in the same house for very long, they're always being passed from hand to hand.

That's why sharing what we have seems right to her – after all, Laureano has always given the three of us the same monthly allowance. Orquídea, though, spends any spare money she has on Ló because, she reckons, she herself doesn't need it. She earns enough money as a cleaner and hopes to earn more later on. She's training to be a nurse, which is good because she likes looking after people. 'Aldemiro is a nurse too. He's very kind, he's going to help me.' No, she doesn't need any money, but Ló does. For books, exercise books, shoes. She's not going to let Ló miss any more school; she's going to tell Fanisse to leave her children with the other wife or with a neighbour, there's no reason why Ló should do it. She'll pull her hair and, if necessary, tear her *capulana;* it'll be hanging from the trees by the time she's finished with her. But Ló is *not* giving up school.

Zedequias isn't well, though, she says with a sigh. He's too old for his wife, too old to work at the docks. He sits on the mat at home, smoking and smoking. The only time he does go out is to push a cart full of fruit, which he sells in the street.

Rodrigo and I sit down opposite each other on the terrace of the Zambi café, which is always full; my chair faces the sea.

His hand reaches out to take mine. Placed together like that, our hands are such different sizes; mine only reaches halfway up his fingers, which now let go of mine, take a cigarette out of the pack and light it. A ring of white smoke hovers in the air for a moment, then rises up and disappears. He takes another puff and breathes out the smoke before saying his first words, leaning towards me over the table.

The sea is the same colour as his eyes. Neither blue nor green, but possibly grey. They're always changing, and you can never be sure.

'What colour *are* your eyes?' I ask, before he can speak.

He laughs and shrugs: after all, he's not the one who spends most time looking at them.

'Café terraces, cinemas, the Baixa, the harbour, the beach. The same places that Laureano used to take me to when I was a child,' I say as if I were talking to myself as I, too, light a cigarette.

It suddenly occurs to me that my father was my first lover. It's always so. But that happened in an unreal, impossible time, lost in the desires and dreams of a childhood that one day got left behind. Somewhere, at the bottom of a cupboard, there's a broken music box with a cat on top that will never dance again.

But this isn't a sad idea, I think, knocking the ash off my cigarette. This is a different time and a different path. As vast as the sea.

The Indian Ocean. I gaze out as far as the horizon, beyond the coconut palms, at the ocean into which flow some of the great rivers of the world, the Indus and the Ganges, the Tigris and the Euphrates, the Limpopo and the Zambezi. It pleases me that the last two names, which are as familiar to me as people, should take their place alongside those other distant, unknown rivers, which evoke other climates and other land-scapes, other suns and other people. The Indian Ocean of the Arabian Sea, the Bay of Bengal, the Red Sea and perhaps others I can no longer recall – the Indian Ocean turned towards the East, to the mysterious, ancient Orient, at once distant and near, that has been arriving on our shores for centuries in the form of ships, Indian silks, Chinese porcelain and Buddhas with eyes fixed and staring into space.

An ocean of warm waters lapping our coast, a sea of coral, fish, molluscs, seaweed and, further off, phosphorescent flying fish.

We smile at each other across the table, both thinking the same thing: where can we be alone?

I look up at the acacias in the street we're walking along now, as if they could provide an answer, as if they could point us to a more sheltered place than that provided by a curtain of foliage.

'The eyes of the city don't care about us,' says Rodrigo. 'People have better things to do than watch us.'

'Yes,' I say, 'that's true.' The people go in and out of Marta da Cruz & Tavares, Orquídea Oriental, Casa Elefante and Bazar Favorito, they read the neon signs on the walls or on top of buildings – 'Kodak Cameras', 'Films', 'Tudor Batteries' – they buy coffee in Rei dos Cafés, breathe in the good smell of camphor in Casa Ho-Lin, stop here and there outside shop windows, go to work, to the markets, to the beach – Blacks, Whites, Indians, Arabs, Chinese, they have their own lives and aren't interested in ours. Besides, given the major events happening in the world, of what possible importance could two lovers be?

Nevertheless, it still doesn't seem to us very easy to just walk into the Hotel Girassol, for example, and ask for a room. The Girassol is always full of people, who go to lunch or dine in the restaurant on the top floor, from where you can see the whole city; no, a smaller, less well-known hotel would be better, for example, the Hotel Central in Rua Araújo. No, that's no good, it has a reputation for being a place frequented by prostitutes. A hotel with no name in a street with no name, but streets with no name and hotels with no name don't exist, and how could we go in and out without it looking strange? Should we take a suitcase with us? Yes, we decide it would be better to arrive in a taxi and let the driver unload the luggage (we'd have to put something in to give it a little weight).

But then how could we leave, only a few hours later, taking our suitcases with us, without having spent the night there? Something unexpected has come up, we would tell the receptionist gravely, returning the key. An act of God. A matter of life and death. But didn't hotels always need some form of identification?

What do other people do, we wonder. Where do they go, which hotels do they use and how do they manage to leave, how do they slip past the receptionist's knowing smile?

What about the Polana, we think. As a last resort. Despite the doubtless exorbitant price. But we don't think about that now, even if we have to spend a whole year's savings on just a few hours in a hotel room.

The Polana. So large and open and full of tourists. It seems to us that among people like that, from all over the world, it would be easy to get lost, to merge discreetly with the guests who wander from the terrace to the bar or simply stand around talking in the various reception rooms. Yes, there is something impersonal and protected about a luxury hotel, where we will be less likely to attract attention. We decide to go there tomorrow. To have a better look at the place, to see what it's like.

And that's what we're doing today. We take a seat in the bar and order a whisky. 'Whisky,' says Rodrigo, adding, even before he's asked: 'and soda.'

'Campari,' I say without hesitation, trying to look confident, crossing my legs and leaning back in the chair.

The table is in a strategic position, where we can see who

enters and who leaves. It was a good idea to come. Besides, it's really nice just being here.

I take a tentative sip of my drink, to see what it tastes like. Not as nice as I imagined. I have never drunk Campari before and only know the name from magazines. I particularly like the colour, but I haven't yet had time to appreciate the taste – the second sip seems sweeter than the first, or at least less bitter.

It's cool inside, air-conditioning presumably, but so quiet you're not even aware of it. A waiter brings a tray with more drinks and places it on the table next to ours, where some businessmen are talking. We hear the clink of glasses or perhaps it's just the clink of ice cubes.

We hear children's laughter outside, probably coming from the swimming pool. But someone tells them to be quiet: Sh, sh! And they stop at once or else move away, because we no longer hear them.

Then, from nearby, comes the unexpected sound of a piano. Without our noticing, a man has sat down and begun to play – light music that forms a pleasant backdrop, barely noticeable, as people talk of other things.

I can't imagine what the bedrooms in the hotel must be like. They're perhaps painted in shades of pale green, with heavy white curtains at the windows. And they'll have bright, luxurious bathrooms with concealed lighting. The wardrobes will have thick, mirrored doors.

The man starts to sing, moving his head slightly closer to the microphone positioned on top of the piano. The music becomes less audible, a mere accompaniment to his voice; his hands run lightly over the keyboard in an ascending scale that gradually fades to nothing.

That's all we would have to do, sit down here, tomorrow or the next day, have a drink and listen to the music, and at some point, get up, slip down the narrow, thickly-carpeted corridors and disappear through the half-open door of a room.

It's easy, we decide, as we walk slowly down the street, heading for the Miradouro. We just have to get past the receptionist and ditch the suitcase – we laugh rather nervously at ourselves. We're a bit frightened because we have no experience of checking in at hotels, but it must be what millions of lovers do, and why should the receptionist care?

'Anyone would think we were planning a crime or a robbery,' Rodrigo says. 'We've studied the lie of the land, checked entrances and exits, observed the habits of the people who live there, all we have to do now is arrange a date and a time and synchronise our watches.' We laugh nervously again – what unforeseen circumstance can we have overlooked?

It isn't as if the eyes of the city were trained on us, we say again, shrugging and taking a deep breath. They're not. It's two or three o'clock in the afternoon, there's little traffic in the streets, nearly everyone is taking their afternoon nap. We lean on the balustrade and look down at the quiet city which, bathed by sun and sea, lies drowsing at our feet.

We walk on a little. Not a soul in sight. Besides, there are never many people here, except on Sundays, when it's full of families, children on bicycles, parked cars. Now, though, there is no one.

We find some shade and sit down beneath the trees. A butterfly lands a few inches from us, striped and brilliant and as big as a fist. It's hot, and a few clouds are building in the sky; beyond the leaves, they drift slowly by.

We watch them as we lie on the scant grass that grows between trees and bushes. We embrace almost without realising it, we glance at each other without speaking, then I close my eyes, feeling his body moving on top of me, like a wave carrying me away.

There is no one else around, not that we care any more. Only we exist, and the rest of the world doesn't matter.

For a few days, nothing else exists. Not even the war.

But afterwards I think: the world is much larger than just us.

'It used to grow in my dreams,' I tell Roberto while we're painting our poster. 'The word tree. It would take nine days to circumnavigate its trunk. And each leaf was as long as the flight of a bird.'

But it didn't only grow in my dreams, it grew in everyone else's dreams too.

The poster is green with large lettering in the centre. Around the letters, we paint a few motifs – coconut palms, the sea, a plantation and a river, although we had originally thought of adding a lake or a waterfall. The image of water seemed to us essential, because this is a country with a lot of water and that fact immediately makes it different. That's why we made the background green, to give an impression of vegetation. In the end, though, we decide against the lake and the waterfall, and opt just for the river, which flows in long esses from one side of the paper to the other.

Underneath the letters, we choose a strong, eye-catching image: tall green grass out of which peers the head of a lion. We copy the lion from the picture that I carry from our living-room wall out to the yard, where we can hide from Rosário's prying eyes and the blare of the radio in the kitchen.

The lion looks equally fierce on the poster, only a little smaller. And its brown hide is slightly lighter in colour. But we think it looks pretty good. Besides, a poster doesn't have to be a work of art.

We meet now in Rodrigo's house because, with time, we have grown bolder, indifferent to the comings and goings of brooms, the roar of vacuum cleaners and the beating of carpets, the light, incessant sound of steps on the stairs or of the garden being watered.

His father arrives home only in time for supper, and the other people in the house are invisible to us because we neither see nor look at them. Or perhaps we are the ones who have become invisible, as if we inhabited another dimension. They may open doors and close windows, clean the glass or wax the floor, be called Joaquim, António or Juliano, but we're not even aware that they exist, we say good morning and good afternoon, smile quickly and almost run past them. Laden with books and papers, we do, of course, have the excuse that we're studying.

That is how I enter the house, without really seeing it, so much so that it takes me a long time to realise just how large it is, and I'm not immediately struck by the lack of light and the heavy, gloomy atmosphere.

Weeks and months will pass before I begin, with surprise, to notice the details: the vast, empty dining room, the bare study with its walls lined with umbila wood, the silver-framed photo of his mother on the writing desk, the oil painting of his father hanging behind the secretaire, the ivory carvings his father has been collecting for several years now, arranged in a glass cabinet; a dresser full of jade miniatures and old coins. And his chief passion, his collection of minerals, all individually labelled and placed in little drawers, fill the shelves lining walls and corridors.

The hum of the air-conditioning. The uniformed servants tiptoeing around. The troubling silence in the rooms, where everything seems dead, catalogued and stored away, as if the house were a museum or a tomb.

His mother sleeping in her rocking-chair, underneath the balcony. That is how Rodrigo has described her to me. She would sometimes fall asleep like that because she could get no rest at night, despite the pills she took. She would occasionally drop off during the day, but would immediately wake up, unless she had been drinking whisky, because she mixed pills and whisky, a dangerous combination.

The sleep of the dead, I think. Dark shadows under her eyes, her hair fallen forward over her face, sticking to her skin with the sweat, saliva dribbling from one corner of her mouth. Leaning back in her rocking chair.

It's as if I had suddenly caught sight of her through a window, sitting on the grass. But I don't want to see her. It makes me squirm, as if I had violated someone's privacy or walked into a room without knocking, even though the door was open. I avert my eyes from the framed photograph of her that Rodrigo has gently turned towards me.

I don't want to stumble across her image again, I think. She's dead, but I'm alive. With time, I'll drive her death out of my thoughts or make the memory fade.

Open the windows, I think later on, as I walk down the street. Let in the sun and the wind. Remake the house anew, reinvent it. In time, the house will be filled with light and laughter again. I'm the next woman in Rodrigo's life. I'm different.

It doesn't occur to me at the time that this is a very opulent house, I simply find it dark and suffocating. And I'm drawn to Rodrigo because he has so little in the world, apart from me.

This, I thought, made me much more precious to him and would make him love me even more.

The little things that set us apart, that make me 'me' and that differentiate him from everyone else – him, Rodrigo, unique, distinct.

I find myself noticing his smallest gestures and even certain banal, external details, like the brand of cigarettes he smokes, the size of his tennis shoes (which we called *sapatilhas*), his favourite colour cotton shirt or the model aircraft he likes to make. Rodrigo doesn't yet know exactly what he wants to do, but whatever career he chooses, he definitely wants to get his pilot's licence, and will probably be a pilot one day. He's still not sure though. And his father's dead set against it.

We leaf through old photograph albums – the house where he lived in Beira, birthday parties, childhood friends, holidays at the beach.

I have a few photographs in my purse as well.

'Didn't Bob Pereira stay at the Polana?' he asks.

'Yes, he did.' Bob Pereira, who could afford expensive hotels and who carried Amélia away with him on a ship.

(Now, though, the image I have of Amélia is almost touching. Or perhaps I just see her differently. I took what was left of her – photos, papers, newspaper cuttings, memories – mixed them all up and refashioned them, until a clear figure finally emerged: a face that I look at and which, in turn, looks at me with large, sad eyes.

She used to sit on the floor and cry. Like a lost child. But no one was to blame, neither Laureano nor me. She wasn't to blame either. It was a sadness that was greater than us and older too. She brought it with her and took it away again when she left. No one could break that sadness. No one was to blame.)

'She has a *lot* of problems.' Lóia's white face making Amélia's black face white. Black and white are variable concepts, I always knew that. Lóia was white. Luminous. She talked about Amélia with something akin to pity, that close companion to understanding: 'She's dead. She's alive, but she's dead.'

They've swapped places now: Lóia is alive, she's part of the wind, the light, the landscape, the soul of this place, one of the familiar spirits we invoke as we stand around the tree of our ancestors. And it's Amélia who's dead, alive and dead, some-where, as if the place she went to – and wherever it was, she never sent word – was also called Mocímboa da Praia.

Roberto doesn't want to leave his *xiluva* sweetheart, but life is driving them apart. Soon he will be going to university, and she hasn't even finished school.

Life separates people without anyone realising it – suddenly everything has changed and nothing is the same. Not even we are the same.

Roberto, though, can't help but feel guilty.

Zedequias certainly doesn't seem the same, I realise when I see him again: his hair has turned white and his baggy shirt flaps about on his scrawny body like clothes hung out to dry in the wind.

'Plenty fruit, *senhora*, plenty fruit,' he says over and over to whoever happens by.

Rolling through the dust in the heat. It's not even a cart really, more like a handcart with two wheels that squeak as he trundles it up the street. He pushes it patiently along – his feet cracked and calloused from walking, the veins in his legs as thick as cables from carrying heavy sacks down at the docks. His hat on his head, his mouth drooping at one corner because of the pipe that he never removes from his lips, even when it's gone out, except to utter his eternal cry, which is always the same the whole morning: 'Plenty fruit, *senhora*, plenty fruit.'

He doesn't use scales, he sells his oranges by the bag, bananas by the dozen or half dozen and pineapples individually. 'Plenty fruit, *senhora*.' A full paper bag and money in exchange. 'Plenty fruit.'

He stops in the shade, sits down for a moment at the back of the cart, wipes the sweat from his brow with the sleeve of his shirt, gets up, again utters his usual cry, waits for a customer to approach or not, waits a little longer, then moves on, struggling to push his cart.

I say goodbye and walk on. He smiles a toothless smile and raises his hand.

That night, I dream of the cart: the swirl of dust on the road, the suffocating heat, the wheels turning and turning, a phrase repeated ad nauseam by a voice. Except that I can't make out the words.

The day when, unexpectedly, we heard a car stop outside in the garden, at four o'clock in the afternoon. Someone (whom we subsequently identified as Juliano) knocked urgently on the bedroom door:

'Master Rodrigo, your father's here.'

We hurriedly get dressed, Rodrigo rushes down the stairs ahead of me, then comes back and has me follow behind him, half-hidden by his body, as far as the kitchen door, which he kicks open, then practically shoves me out into the yard at the back.

'Quick,' he whispers, then immediately closes the door and disappears into the house.

The street is only two steps away, a small, quiet street at the rear of the house, where there is no garden, only the washing-line and a few square feet of neglected ground.

I stand there for a moment, not knowing if the arrival of his father was pure chance or intentional; I wait to see his father peer out of a window; I listen for voices, but hear nothing.

He probably doesn't even know I exist, I think. But I wouldn't care if he did; I have grown in confidence over time.

I stand there watching, but no one comes to the windows.

Rosário is, once again, at the gate, talking to the same man of a few days ago, and to whom she bids a hasty farewell as soon as she catches sight of me.

'What's the problem?' I ask good-humouredly, opening the door. 'Are you embarrassed to have a boyfriend?'

She doesn't reply, but angrily mutters something, snatches

off her scarf and, for no apparent reason, starts pacing back and forth between the kitchen and the living-room, as if the house were a cage.

I go to my room, and a moment later, the radio starts up. Too loud, as usual.

'What a shame you couldn't have stayed outside talking to your boyfriend,' I think with a sigh.

I try to immerse myself in a book, but can't concentrate, not even with my hands over my ears. I read the same page ten times, unable to get any further.

'Turn the radio down!' I yell, flinging open the door to my room.

It seems she doesn't hear me because the music continues to blare forth. I go out onto the landing and shout:

'Rosááááriiiooo! I can't concentrate. Don't you understand? Turn the music down, all right?'

'Sorry,' she says from the kitchen in the most innocent of voices and lowers the volume.

The music gradually becomes audible again, softly at first, then rises by degrees until it's at full blast, pounding inside my head.

I race down the stairs and burst into the kitchen. Rosário takes fright and drops a tray of glasses that shatter on the tiles.

'That's your fault,' I shout above the din. 'But enough is enough. You can only have that music on when I'm not in the house.' (I should have done this ages ago, I think, as I pick up the radio. I must be a complete idiot.)

She makes as if to sweep up the broken glass, but instead stands there, playing with the broom.

'I like loud music,' she says at last in an offended tone of voice. 'He gave me that radio. Your father. There was loud music where I worked as a waitress.'

'Where?'

'In the bar.'

'What bar?' I ask with a shudder. 'In Araújo?'

'No,' she says, 'in the centre. In the Baixa. I used to serve drinks, the music was always loud. I like it loud.'

'Well, I don't,' I say, taking the radio and closing the door behind me.

'He suspects something,' says Rodrigo. 'That's why he came home in the middle of the afternoon. I expect one of them gave us away.'

This doesn't seem plausible to me. Why wouldn't António, Juliano or Joaquim be on our side, always assuming there are two sides? And why would Rodrigo's father necessarily be against us?

Besides, if Juliano warned us once, he would warn us again, it was an unspoken, unbreakable agreement. 'Anyway, I don't want to think about your father,' I say.

For a while, we again forget that he exists.

After some thought, Roberto decides that it's not a good idea to put our poster underneath the other one (we now know that the band playing at the dance will be Shegundo Galarza). On the night, people's thoughts are going to be on other things and they'll be on too much of a high even to notice our poster, he says.

And so another night, long before the dance, we go and attach our poster to the door of the school.

The following morning, however, it's not there. To our great disappointment, no one mentions it; probably no one even saw it, apart from the first person to arrive, who immediately tore it down.

By then, it would certainly have been ripped to pieces – the plantation, the river with its long esses, the head of the lion peering out. All that work lost, as if it had never existed. The only proof that it did once exist are the smudgy marks left on the glass panes by the glue.

Rosário went into a sulk after that incident with the radio. She's angry with me, and when I arrive home in the afternoon, she pretends not to notice me and stays where she is, sitting in the aviator's chair, painting her nails. She has her scarf tied about her head again and one sandal dangles from her toes when she crosses her legs, yawning.

'It's hot,' she says at last, blowing on her nails.

Clearly no one came home for lunch, because the breakfast things are still on the table, and two flies are buzzing round the empty cups. Smears of jam have congealed on the plates and a watery black liquid has oozed out of the filter full of coffee grounds and made a large, irregular stain on the cloth.

On the sideboard, a bunch of faded flowers sits in a vase. I carry it into the kitchen, throw the flowers in the bin, empty out the putrid water, then add some soap and scrub away at the layer of green slime in the bottom of the vase.

I do all this as slowly as possible, trying to gain time before I say anything. I count up to twenty, then up to fifty. Rosário has apparently done nothing all day, apart from paint her nails: the saucepans sit empty on the bench, and there are three pairs of shoes and a lone stiletto on the floor, along with brushes, washing-up cloths and bits of newspaper.

I go back into the room and face her. My voice is very calm.

'What's up with you?' I ask.

She puts the brush back in the bottle of nail varnish and stretches lazily:

'It's so hot,' she says at last, without even looking at me.

Days later, though, she looks me straight in the eye when she spins round on her heels:

'I've fallen pregnant by him,' she says, as if she were announcing a new world order.

'Who do you mean?' I ask distractedly, almost automatically. Because I don't know Rosário's boyfriends and, besides, I couldn't care less who got her pregnant.

'Your father,' she says, opening her eyes very wide and bursting into surprised laughter. 'In seven months' time, he have a new baby.'

'I must be completely blind,' I say to Roberto. 'How could I not have realised earlier. That's obviously why he brought her to the house. How could I not have seen that?'

Now I see it — all too clearly. (A bird that fell from the tree because it didn't open its wings in time. And then all you have to do is reach out and pick it up. Just reach out your hand.)

A child as life insurance. Because he'll take care of them both, of course, support them for ever. Even if he has to look after the house and the child on his own, and she'll continue to flirt with whoever comes to the gate or the window and one day swap Laureano for one of those passers-by.

'Why her?' sighs Bibila, shaking her head. 'Why did he have to choose her?'

'What did you expect?' asks Roberto. 'Some people are good and some people aren't. I don't see why you're so surprised.'

(Sitting in his aviator's chair as if he were sleeping with his eyes open — old-fashioned glasses, white hair, and that sad, distant, absorbed look.

All you had to do was reach out your hand and pick up the bird where it lay on the ground.)

All day I repeat over and over to myself: There's nothing I can do.

There's nothing anyone can do.

'He's going to repeat the whole sorry story,' I say to Jamal and

Bibila. 'But I don't want to be here to watch it happen all over again. Not again, please God. Not again.'

I could leave home and move in with Rodrigo. A small apartment, however small, would be enough for us.

But that's not possible. There's only one way out, I think in desperation. My cousins' house. In Lisbon.

But I shudder at the mere thought because I don't want to go to Lisbon. Nor do I want to leave Rodrigo.

We're walking slowly down the street beneath the trees. Rodrigo's arm is round my shoulders and my arm is round his waist.

'I've fallen pregnant by you,' I say suddenly, without thinking.

That's what I say, because Rosário's words are still dancing around inside my head and because I feel like saying it, just for a joke, to see how he'll react to that lie and to my revelation of the truth immediately afterwards. It's just a game, one of the many games love plays. He'll be surprised, incredulous, slightly frightened, but all the reactions I foresee include, above all, a large dose of tenderness.

Suddenly, I almost regret that it isn't true. As if just saying those words had placed a child inside my womb.

For a moment, that child exists simply because I spoke – it's there between us, between our embracing arms, between our two bodies walking along together.

Rodrigo, however, immediately shrinks back from me, his face contracts into a grimace and he grows pale.

'It's not true,' I say, but he hurls me against the wall, shakes me violently by the shoulders, as if he had gone mad.

'It's not true,' I say again, feeling frightened and sorry I ever spoke.

He doesn't hear me, though, he doesn't want to hear me;

his face is deathly pale and his eyes bright with panic and rage.

'You did it on purpose,' he yells. 'On purpose. To ruin my life.'

When I try to reach out for his hands, he grabs my arms, squeezes them brutally as if to crush an enemy, then propels me backwards and walks, no, almost runs away without even looking at me.

The letter the next day. With sentences like stones.

(His father used to shout: 'Now you listen to me.' And his mother would cover her ears so as not to hear, but he would hammer the words into her head, each one harder than the last, as if he wanted to crack open her head. 'Now you listen to me.')

Now you listen to me: 'I was never sure about my feelings for you.' 'I still have no idea what I want really.' 'The innocence of youth, on your part and on mine.' 'Besides, we couldn't have gone on like that.' 'It would have to have ended at some point.'

(His father hurls a stone at his mother's head, and she starts to bleed, above her eyebrows and in the middle of her forehead. The blood dribbles from her ears).

'If there's any problem, I'm sure we can find a solution.' 'My father will pay all the expenses.' 'We know a good doctor.' 'In South Africa.'

Like stones. Like knives. A knife in his mother's mouth to shut her up, in each of her eyes so that she won't see, in her heart so that she won't feel, a knife in the belly to make their child disappear, disappear quickly. For ever.

When I re-read the letter, it occurs to me that perhaps the letter was dictated, because it doesn't sound like him. But it's his writing and he signed it: Rodrigo.

Even his name has become a stone.

Along with the letter came a bunch of roses.

I throw them in the bin, along with the letter torn into pieces.

This shocks and surprises Rosário. That night, I find the flowers in a vase in my room, just as they arrived, wrapped in cellophane and still with the florist's card attached.

'You can't throw away pretty roses like that,' she says from where she stands in the doorway.

'Don't you dare touch them,' I scream, again throwing the flowers into the kitchen bin.

I need to talk to Rodrigo. To explain to him and to let him explain to me.

'Master Rodrigo isn't home,' says António's voice on the phone. 'He's gone to Beira with his father.'

During the weeks that follow, he doesn't come to any classes. And when I phone, Joaquim, António or Juliano always say that Master Rodrigo is not at home. He's staying in Beira. With his godparents.

What's the phone number there?

They don't have a phone.

In the end, I write to him:

'It's not true. There is no baby.' 'But if there was, neither you nor your father would make the decision for me as to whether or not it would live.'

'But it's good we had that conversation because I found out who you really are.' 'And now that I know you, I never want to see you again.'

'Tell your father to spend his money on himself and go and see a doctor in South Africa or wherever,' and I add, 'a doctor for the insane.' 'And you'd better go too, because you're turning out to be just like him.'

I hesitate, my pen in my hand. I'm not sure if I'm going to stop because I've said all I need to say or if I've only just begun and I'm going to continue and never ever stop.

Suddenly I find that I've filled a whole page and another and another and another – a long letter for a very long anger.

('Your father will pay all the expenses. Just so that you and he can get rid of me quickly – through the back door.') ('Did you think I wanted a child as some kind of life insurance?') ('Do you really believe you're worth more than me?')

I re-read what I've written, but have difficulty in making out the words: a lot of sentences were crossed out, replaced by others, and with new ones written between the lines, the writing is all over the place, quite shaky sometimes, and the paper is crumpled and tear-stained.

Exhausted, my head spinning, I realise that I'm going to have to copy out the whole wretched thing. In the end, though, I give up. I'll leave just the first few sentences, I decide. I'm too tired, and the effort of writing, now that I've made it, seems entirely pointless.

I won't say anything more. Only the first part. It seems to me that aggression might be interpreted as a desire for contact, for some reaction. And just then I don't want any reaction from Rodrigo. I want a deep, clean cut, leaving no root.

And that was precisely what happened. Rodrigo never came looking for me, never even phoned.

He missed what classes he could and only really turned up again for the final exams. And he walked past me as if he didn't know me, as if he had never known me.

That was when we decided to write the message in charcoal on the outside of the school. So that they wouldn't forget. Because the war was a long way off and life in the city went on unchanged, as if nothing had happened. We settled on a Sunday night, when there would be no one else in the street.

Even so, we would have to be quick because the occasional car might pass and we were afraid of the police.

Roberto would write 'Independence for' and I would write 'Mozambique' followed by an exclamation mark.

I had got as far as the 'q' when we spotted headlights at the end of the street. I finished the word off as best as I could, then hid behind the nearest tree. (I could hardly deny it if they caught me because my hands and clothes and probably my face, too, were smeared with charcoal.

'Good God,' I thought, my heart beating faster as the car approached, 'if even writing a few words on a wall is this complicated, how are we ever going to change the world?)

When we arrived the next morning, we saw that the exclamation mark was slightly crooked and a few inches below the words, but the words – praise God – were there.

'The cart won't go,' says Ló on Sunday. 'One of the wheels is broken. He just sits on the mat now and smokes and smokes.'

(He's done everything and he's tired now. Death has its uses.)

(A wheel turning in space. We push and push, and the cart of life won't move, until suddenly a wheel springs off and crushes us.)

I would like to believe, I think, looking at Laureano through the half-open door (he unfolds the newspaper, cleans his glasses on his handkerchief and, once he's put them back on, immerses himself patiently in his reading, making a slight rustling sound as he turns the pages), I would like to believe that he could be happy with Rosário, that a child could be a new beginning.

But he's already let the newspaper fall and is dozing, looking lost and absent, his glasses still perched on his nose, as he sits in his aviator's chair, mouth half-open, head lolling back.

It's a Sunday afternoon, a dead Sunday afternoon.

Rosário has gone out and is perhaps strolling around in Xipamanine with the postman. Or else at the beach.

'Never give up on life, whatever happens,' I think as I watch him sleeping. 'Never give up.'

But he gave up long ago. A lot of people can't take it and simply give up, not through any fault of their own, but because they're pursued by some injustice, a wheel that suddenly crushes them. If you don't escape in time, if you don't manage to escape in time.

(Zedequias waving to me in the street. His toothless smile, that brief gesture with his hand.

The *xiluva* sweetheart left behind – running down a road, running, but the road is so long, so very long. You can't see where it ends, and she's so tired. And the road is getting emptier and emptier.)

'If you want to get on with your life, don't worry,' says Jamal. 'We'll keep an eye on him. André and Relito, myself and Bibila.'

'I want to go to university in Lisbon,' I say to Laureano one night. I drop the words into the conversation, as if they were of no consequence.

He looks at me, surprised, and for a few days says nothing. He seems more tired and depressed than usual. Then he asks:

'Are you sure you want to go there?'

'Yes, I'm sure,' I say. (I have no alternative, I think. But I don't say that.)

A letter was dispatched to Narciso. And shortly afterwards back came the reply:

'Your cousins share a room and each accuses the other of being the untidy one. Anyway, to avoid adding a third person to create still more chaos, Gita can stay in the other room, with my sister-in-law Isilda. She's Josina's sister and helps around the house.'

'That's it, then,' I think. 'That's it.' The cousin from Africa will, of course, have to help around the house as well, and just to make this absolutely clear we're offering her a bed in the room of the other woman who helps around the house, because obviously any outsider being taken in as a favour, so to speak, has no rights and must earn her bread by serving the insiders.

That narrow, torpid life, the lack of air and space in the country that is my cousins' house. Unfortunately, I have no alternative. I have no alternative.

An ill-governed country. Badly run. But it could be blown apart, be forced to rethink everything. The Old Man was on his throne, but surely we could knock him off it.

Live and you will see. And I'm going to live. And I'll see that country-that-is-my-cousins'-house either explode or implode.

Isilda's poky little room. I can imagine it full of lace doilies and glass vases and images of saints.

But that's just at the beginning, because there must be some work for me in Lisbon – as a waitress or a shop assistant, in an office, a grocery store or a boutique, something that will pay for my studies and guarantee my independence.

Independence, I repeat, fascinated, as if I hadn't realised until then that this was what it was all about:

One day, all of a sudden, you're free, and you no longer depend on anyone else.

Give my share to Orquídea, I tell Laureano, meaning my allowance. She always spends hers on Ló; or rather, share it out among the three of them. (Because there's going to be another child, and we'll have to make room for it.)

But I'm outside all of that now. Independent. Like this country. And at the same time too.

I smile at the thought of our poster and the words we scrawled on the wall.

The sound of Africa, I think, picking up a dried *maçala* fruit, putting it to my ear and hearing the seeds inside rattle. The sound of Africa, near and far. Like a conch shell.

I put it in my suitcase. I'll take it with me (because suddenly it's my last day in Lourenço Marques, my suitcase is packed and open on my bed).

I go out to buy a few things, but I'm in a hurry, it's only a few hours until night.

(A night flight, a bat-flight — a great metal ship racing down the runway, then suddenly lifting into the air and leaving.

They always fly at night, says Joana. They wake you at six or seven in the morning to force-feed you some breakfast, unless you warn the stewardess that you don't want to be woken. You wake feeling a complete wreck, from having slept in your seat with a blanket over your knees and your head bumping against the window whenever it slips off the pillow. Wear a woollen jacket or a sweater because it's often really cold on planes.)

Then I pop into the Zambi café for a quick coffee with Roberto. I show him the little hand-crafted gifts I've bought and unwrap them on the table.

'Do you think they'll like them?'

(The world that I'm leaving behind. Rivers, plantations, savannahs, palm groves, wide open spaces, broad horizons, and a tree that used to grow in my dreams and that reached up to the sky – what do they know of all that, how can they understand?

The cousin from Africa, who has experienced different things and comes from a place where the people speak a hybrid language, in which the grammar breaks down because they think differently and thinking has to be left free to happen, what do they know about that, what do they know?)

'I'm going to feel suffocated in Lisbon,' I say.

He smiles and wraps up my packages for me again.

'Don't give up.'

'Don't give up,' I say to him as well. 'Never give up.'

(And with that our conversation ends. Because now our paths will diverge. After years of sharing almost everything.)

'I'll walk you home.'

When we arrive, he stops outside, on the other side of the street, and embraces me.

'I'll wait here until you've gone in.'

(Until you disappear. Until you disappear into the night, into the dark.)

At the door, I turn and wave. But I can't see him because my eyes are full of rain, and night has suddenly fallen. Like an eyelid closing.